When the Cooper famil
Donegal, Brian is unhap
settle into his new life o
two cousins, Laura and
bridge the gap of loneliness.

Unwittingly he is drawn into a deeper drama – that of the enigmatic Susannah Parry, her son Richard, and their troubled family history.

Then one dark October evening, Brian goes up the tangled overgrown avenue of Ashbrook, the old Parry house.

What he finds there will change his life dramatically …

Yvonne MacGrory

The Ghost of
SUSANNAH PARRY

Illustrated by Terry Myler

THE CHILDREN'S PRESS

First published 1995 by
The Children's Press
45 Palmerston Road, Dublin 6
Reprinted 1996

ISBN 0 947962 90 5

Typesetting by Computertype Limited
Printed by Colour Books Limited

For my father
Sonny

My father was a great story-teller, and as a child I used to find his ghost stories, with their mixture of truth and fantasy, particularly fascinating.
Even today I love a good ghost story – and there are plenty still being told here in Donegal.

Contents

1
Fernhill

It was the sound of his own scream that had awakened him. It still hung in the air around, faintly ringing in his ears. This was the second night he had woken, drenched in sweat and his heart pounding, because of some unknown terror. The bedclothes were in a tangled mess and his pillows lay on the floor some distance from the bed, where he must have flung them from him in panic. He had no memory of switching on the bedside light which revealed the disarray.

Discarding his top sheet and retrieving his pillows, Brian Cooper switched off the small round lamp and lay there thinking, the light from the crescent moon falling across his face. His heart had stopped its loud pounding, but he still had a vague feeling of anxiety and sleep eluded him. He tried to piece together the dream which came to him in tantalizing snatches. It was the same dream both nights. He had been running, his breath coming in short agonised bursts. Just thinking about it was enough to make his breathing become more rapid again.

He had been running down stairs at first. That much he knew. But they were not the stairs in his house. No, they were wider and there was something peculiar in the background too, some odd detail that he could not remember. But he did remember being afraid. Terribly afraid.

Luckily no one seemed to have heard his scream, probably because his bedroom was at the front of the house, separated from the others by stairs and a small landing. He could just imagine his mother's comment, and silently in the dark he mouthed the familiar words. 'It's just the reaction of your unconscious to moving house, Brian.' And she would probably be right, because he had hating moving from Dublin. He had never really told his mother and father how he felt, but they were so excited and so delighted to be moving that he had said nothing, thinking that maybe everything would be all right once he got here. But it was even worse than he expected. He missed his friends, and he missed the city noises and the familiar buildings. Here he was surrounded by hills and heather and prickly whin bushes. Dublin was his city. He could not see himself settling into country life.

As he turned again, away from the cold menacing moon, shutting out his dream, he could hear his father's voice saying encouragingly, 'Donegal is a beautiful county, and we're not far from Donegal town or even Sligo. We can visit Letterkenny often, and I will have to go into Derry sometimes. It's a beautiful city.'

He quickly closed his eyes to block out the memory of the hurt look that had come across his father's face when he had refused to join the rest of the family on that first trip to Letterkenny.

He was not getting along with his father the way he used to. They were unable to talk to each other at the moment. All his father seemed interested in was getting back to Donegal, 'home', as he called it.

Home? It wasn't his home and never would be.

Brian struggled awake next morning to the sound of his

mother's constant calling. His eyes were gritty, his limbs leaden, his movements sluggish and clumsy while he was dressing. He didn't think the school uniform of navy jumper and trousers, blue shirt and red tie too bad, but he much preferred the grey and wine of his old school in Dublin. He wouldn't have to bother with a jacket today as it was a dry morning.

His father and mother, Ian and Sheila, looked up when he came into the kitchen. 'You should have been up earlier to set the table,' said Sheila as he sat down to breakfast. 'And you're getting circles under your eyes – earlier to bed for you in future.'

'If he would spend less time playing with that Game Boy …' There was obvious disapproval in Ian's voice.

'Well, there isn't anything else to do here,' Brian replied sullenly.

'You haven't made much of an effort to find something else to do since we arrived, have you?'

The two Cooper girls giggled. Cliona was tall for her twelve years and had blue eyes like her mother. Niamh, who was on the chubby side, had green eyes like Ian, and both girls had long blonde hair.

Paul was not paying any attention to the others. At six years of age he was the youngest of the family, and this morning he was spooning his Weetabix as if it were the last bite he'd see that day. He was the only one of the children with freckles, and his hair was straight and fair like Brian's.

After breakfast, as the children were piling into the car, Sheila spoke quietly to her husband: 'Ian, do give Brian a chance to adapt. He's finding it all very strange, with the new school and everything.'

'You would think he knew nothing at all about living in

the country. He has absolutely no interest in his new surroundings,' said Ian in disgust.

'Well, the countryside looks a lot different when you're on holiday, for a couple of weeks in the summer. Brian used to love it, but he was so much younger than. Anyway, Ian, do try to remember that Brian still misses his friends,' Sheila reminded him none too gently.

'Right, right,' sighed Ian, and giving Sheila a quick kiss he promised to be more patient. But when he got into the car and saw his oldest son sitting in the front seat, his narrow shoulders hunched, head bowed, silently contemplating the floor, his good resolve nearly vanished.

After waving good-bye to the family Sheila went indoors again and poured herself another cup of tea. Normally she would enjoy a few pages of whatever book she was currently reading before tackling the chores, but this morning she could not settle down as usual. She was worried about Brian; he was not adapting to their new way of life as she and Ian had hoped.

When Ian's grand-uncle Peter had died and left him this house it had come as a complete surprise, but Ian had spent many happy holidays at Fernhill as a child, and Peter knew how he loved the place. The house had been let for years, as the old man, who had developed Alzheimer's, had gone to a nursing home outside Letterkenny. Ian used to visit him there in the beginning, but it upset him so much when his grand-uncle did not know him that he stopped going.

Gradually he had lost touch with Donegal, and when he married and the children came along they had spent holidays with Sheila's mother in Wicklow.

When Peter died, the Coopers had travelled to Donegal

for the funeral. And it was when Jack, Ian's cousin, introduced them to the local solicitor outside the beautiful old
stone church in Rossmore that Ian learned he was the new
owner of Fernhill. They called to Mr Cassidy's office after
the funeral for the house keys and the solicitor promised to
get the paperwork sorted out during the coming weeks.
Straightway they decided to drive out and take a look at
the house before returning to Dublin.

That had been at the beginning of April and it was a
cold day with heavy showers, but as they drove out of
Rossmore, passing clumps of waving daffodils and patches
of pale yellow primroses sheltering in the hedges, both
Sheila and Ian had experienced a feeling of deep con-
tentment.

Further on the countryside became wild and bleak, the
road bordered on one side by low stunted bushes and on
the other by the Atlantic. Ian stopped the car at a sheltered
cove just past a small white-washed cottage and they
watched in fascination as the white-crested waves crashed
against the side of a towering rock jutting into the sea.

'Beautiful, isn't it,' Ian said as they drove inland again,
past the budding rowan trees and the hawthorn hedges
which were breaking into small green leaf. In the sloping
fields of varied green, the little lambs were white against
the darker fleece of the mothers. It made Sheila's hands
itch to get at her brushes. She must get down to painting
again, now the children were at school.

And then they were driving down the gravelled laneway
lined with arching evergreen trees, and when Ian drew up
in front of the white two-storied house they sat for a
moment as Ian pointed out the tall cypress-tree where a
swing used to hang when he was a child, the barn with
uneven steps leading up to its red-painted door, the gate

leading into the yard, the half-neglected garden. Then they went in and walked around the house, and Ian relived some of his happiest memories.

Sheila had been to Fernhill years before and had loved the place from the first moment she saw it. Now it was theirs! But what a pity to have to sell it. Her eyes met Ian's and almost together they had cried, in a moment of complete euphoria, 'Why not move here?'

They planned their move on the journey back to Dublin. Ian, who was a free-lance journalist, could work just as easily from the country, and perhaps now he would get the time and peace to settle down to write the novel he had been planning for so long.

And for Sheila, who was an artist, the barn could quite easily be converted into a large studio. The thought of having so much space for herself and her painting appealed to her hugely. It had all seemed so perfect. The children, they were sure, would love Fernhill, and when they all went up for a week-end to see it, Cliona and Niamh had been ecstatic, a little worried at first about leaving their friends but reassured when told they could have them up to visit, and that, anyway, they would now be making new friends. Paul had run around the garden spotting wildlife, beaming all over.

In retrospect, maybe Brian had been unusually quiet. But in the general excitement neither Ian nor Sheila had thought it significant, putting it down to teenage reluctance to enthuse about anything the rest of the family was going overboard about.

Plans had been put in hand immediately and Jack was a great help, recommending tradesmen and builders' suppliers, and Ian went to Donegal every couple of weeks to see how the work was progressing. The move had been planned for mid-August, to give the children time to settle in before starting their new schools. But the repairs and renovations were not finished by then so it was postponed until September. They had had no trouble selling their Dublin house: a buyer had appeared almost as soon as they put it on the market.

Sheila would never forget the day they actually moved and the contents of four vans were unloaded. It was sheer chaos – a chaos that reigned for a number of days. Jack and Paula had been terrific, with Jack helping to carry furniture upstairs (and often downstairs again) and Paula providing delicious hot stews, made in her own house and reheated in the microwave.

They were very happy with the results of the renovations they had made to Fernhill. They had replaced the small windows with larger ones to let more light into the low-ceilinged rooms and they had knocked two small rooms into one, which they used as part sitting- and part dining-room, although mainly the family ate in the large kitchen. There was a large room at the back of the house which Ian and Sheila decided to use as their study. Cliona and Niamh had a couple of arguments about the decoration of their bedroom, which was the largest since they were sharing – Cliona wanted green, Niamh blue – but in the end they compromised on a sunny primrose yellow and both were delighted with the result. Paul had the small bedroom beside his parents and had been promised that he could pin up all his Man Utd posters.

Sheila had not been unduly worried that Brian showed such a lack of interest when she was selecting paint and curtains for his bedroom. But then he usually ended up covering the walls with posters of heavy metal groups, whose ripped jeans left Ian scratching his head in bewilderment. In his young day such tattered garments would have been dumped long ago; now it seemed they were style.

Looking back, Sheila could see that Brian had been moody and quietly rebellious ever since the move to Fernhill. He hadn't wanted to help Ian to put up a new swing for Paul on the cypress-tree. He hadn't taken part in the mammoth gardening clean-up she had organised with their own family and Jack and Paula's and a few of their friends. He had become more and more uncommunicative. Never very voluble, he only spoke now at meals when someone asked him a question. But she and Ian had been so caught up in their own day-to-day plans and activities that they had never sat down, talked to him and asked him if there were any problems. They would have to put that right.

Sheila poured herself another cup of tea and thought how perfect it would all be – if only Brian was his old self again.

2

A Missing Document

Ian was humming tunelessly to himself as they drove the mile and a half to Rossmore. Cliona, Niamh and Paul soon broke in with chatter about school and the new friends they were making. As he listened to them Brian wished he could make friends that easily, but he just wasn't like that and he did miss Jonathen and Rory. Michael, who was Jack and Paula's son, had taken him under his wing, but he had two best friends, Kieran and David, and it seemed to Brian that they resented Michael being friendly towards him. They were all around thirteen, his own age.

'Brian,' Ian's voice interrupted his thoughts, 'I've asked Barney Flood to come to the house this evening. He was a neighbour of Peter's in the old days and I met him as a child. Wouldn't have known him if Jim Rogers hadn't told me who he was. Anyway, I introduced myself. I'm going to ask him to tell me a few of his father's stories about some of the characters who used to live around here. I may do an article about them. Would you like to come along and listen to him?'

'Great,' Brian replied, with no real show of enthusiasm. Ian sighed. All very well for Sheila to counsel patience but it was difficult with such a lack of response.

They had cut it a bit fine this morning and Brian just made it to his class before the bell went. Michael had kept a seat for him and he grinned as Brian slid breathlessly down beside him. They had two classes of Irish in the morning. Another plus as far as his parents were concerned about moving to Donegal was their close proximity to the Donegal Gaeltacht. Brian liked the musical sing-song quality of some of the pupils' voices as they read the words of Mairtin Ó Direain from his poem *Bás*.

Bas	Death
Chonaic me faoilean	I saw a seagull
Ag eitilt o dheas	Flying south
Thar na craga amach	Out over the rocks
Is rud in a bheal.	And something in his mouth.
Bhi Peadar Phaidin	Paddy Peter was
Basaithe o mhaidin.	Dead since morning.
Anam Pheadair Phaidin	Paddy Peter's soul
A bhi mbeal an ein,	Was in the bird's mouth,
Is e a thabairt	And he was taking it
Chun na flaithis,	To the heavens,
A deir mo mhathair.	My mother said.

They had English class before lunch and Miss Bonner gave them back their corrected essays. 'I found them rather disappointing,' she said. '*Macbeth* is a really interesting play about ambition and conscience and how people change under pressure. But most of you just skimmed the surface and wrote about the witches as if they were Hallowe'en extras. However, there was one very good essay. Brian wrote about Banquo's ghost, making the point that the ghost is not, as many people believe, a figment of Macbeth's imagination. In those days people, especially in a wild place like Scotland, really did believe in ghosts ...

Well done, Brian, that was an excellent effort. Highly original. You must read it to us tomorrow – there isn't time now I'm afraid.'

Brian reddened. He knew his essay would not have been as good if Sheila hadn't known Shakespeare backwards and talked so much about his plays, especially *Macbeth*. But he was rather glad the teacher liked it and he was quite pleased with himself until he heard David and Kieran speaking in the seat behind him.

'Just because he's from Dublin, thinks he knows everything,' David muttered loudly to Kieran.

'Maybe we should introduce him to our own local ghost,' sneered Kieran.

'Don't pay any attention to them,' advised Michael when he saw Brian about to turn in his seat to confront them.

'They don't like me much, do they?' Brian remarked as he was walking up the town with Michael at lunch-time.

'They don't know you yet. Give them time.' Michael defended his friends.

A shout from behind made them look around and David joined them. 'Are you going to Gallaghers for chips, Michael?' he asked, ignoring Brian. 'Kieran's gone to grab a table.'

'Yes, okay,' Michael agreed, explaining to Brian that of the four chip shops in town Gallaghers gave the best value for money.

'Michael, over here,' Kieran called when Michael and Brian got their chips.

'Brian is going to sit with us,' said Michael firmly when he joined his friends.

'Oh, I didn't realise that was Brian. I though maybe it was his ghost,' smirked Kieran.

'Brian believes in ghosts. Don't you, Brian?' asked David.

'I'm not sure ...' began Brian

'Maybe we could arrange for him to meet one. Should we tell him about Susannah Parry?' whispered David loudly to Kieran.

'Maybe a visit to her house would give him material for another essay on ghosts.' The boys laughed together.

'Why don't we talk about something else,' Michael said, glaring at his friends.

'I don't mind,' said Brian. 'I take it there's a house locally that's haunted. That's the usual thing, isn't it? But most ghost stories are just a load of rubbish. For every one that might be genuine, there are hundreds that are dreamed up because of old stories about murders and violence. Add creaking floor-boards or squeaking doors and – you have a ghost! I think country people are more superstitious about these things than city people,' he added, wincing loudly when Michael kicked him on the ankle under the table.

'He thinks we live in the dark ages up here,' said David, winking at Kiernan who was sniggering. '*My* ghost is for real. Yours is just an overheated imagination ... Come on, let's go.'

'No, no, I didn't mean that at all,' Brian tried to explain to the retreating backs of the boys as they got up, pushed back their chairs and went to the door. Even Michael seemed annoyed with him and hurried ahead with the others.

Michael had forgotten his temporary irritation after school and offered Brian a lift home in their car. The school bus service only catered for pupils who lived more than two miles from the school, so those who lived nearer either walked home or got a lift, depending on car and parent availability. Brian thought he might start taking his bike on good days.

Michael's older sister Laura sat in the front of the car with her mother. She was a tall serious girl with auburn hair, and like her brother she had a scattering of freckles across her nose, which she hated. She was in her second year. Usually second-years didn't bother much with first-years, but she gave Brian a warm friendly smile which he immediately responded to.

Paula Doherty was a homely, chatty woman and Brian agreed politely when she enthused about the beauty of Rossmore and the surrounding area. Laura chimed in only once, when she said they were passing one of her favourite spots. And Brian liked what he saw too, when he looked down at the gentle curve of a small sandy beach, two large row-boats upturned on the smooth sand, and gazed further out at the stormy sea crashing against the rocks under a darkening sky.

Paula dropped him off at his laneway and, thanking them, Brian hurried off as the heavy raindrops began to fall.

Brian rushed his homework and was ready after tea when Barney was due to call. But he didn't turn up.

'Must have forgotten,' grumbled Ian, 'and I was hoping for a few stories – I have a deadline tomorrow. Come on, Brian. We'll go down to Magees. That's where I ran into him last week. We might be lucky.'

In spite of his non-commital reply that morning, Brian had been looking forward to meeting Barney, as his father had told him some of the famous stories at second-hand. So he followed Ian out to the car.

Barney was indeed in Magees, standing by the counter. Brian wondered if he was imaging it or had a faint look of unease crossed his face when they both came in.

'We were expecting you at Fernhill. You promised you'd drop in tonight,' said Ian.

'Must have forgotten,' mumbled Barney.

'No harm done. We can talk here. What are you having? A Guinness?'

'No, thanks. Never more than one.'

As he looked at the tall heavy-set man with the bushy beard and the watery pale-blue eyes, now narrowed in concentration as he got his pipe going to his satisfaction, Brian thought Barney too old to wear his white hair, which curled over the collar of his tweed jacket, so long.

'Barney,' Ian began, 'I'm thinking of doing an article on some of the old characters your father used to tell you about. I'd love you to tell me a few of those stories. We could start now if that's okay, and I could record them. I wouldn't print them without your permission first of course.'

'Well, I'd like to help if I can,' said Barney slowly.

'There was one story in particular you used to tell about the old fellow who lived in a barrel. I remember you telling me that one when I was a child. Your father used to call him the Diogenes of Rossmore. It took me years to discover who Diogenes was,' Ian laughed remembering.

'Who was Diogenes anyway?' Brian asked.

'A Greek philosopher who lived a simple life! He refused to have any material possessions, so he lived in a tub. Used to walk around in the daytime carrying a lighted lantern. When asked why, he would say, "I'm looking for an honest man." '

It seemed to Brian that Barney had become increasingly restless. He wondered if Ian had noticed, but he seemed unaware of the tension and kept on talking. 'What on earth was that old fellow's name? He lived outside Rossmore somewhere.'

'Sorry. I can't think of it.'

'And then there was the story about the fellow who caught a banshee. Remember how we used to laugh about that. Tell us that one.'

But Barney was turning away. 'I can't bring it to mind. Maybe some other time,' he muttered. Leaving his drink half finished, he took his hat from the counter and left.

'Well! What a way to behave! Did I say something to upset him, do you think?' Ian was genuinely puzzled.

'I don't know. He *did* seem very uneasy,' said Brian, disappointed by his sudden departure.

'Barney used to love an audience. I don't understand it.'

Sheila had a ready explanation. 'Probably he's forgotten the stories completely. After all, he is rather old now. He may be too embarrassed to admit his memory is not what it used to be. And, remember, you did take him by surprise.'

'No, we had arranged the meeting. He forgot that too.'

'Proves my point. It's just old age.'

'That could be it. He looks so fit that I forget he's getting on in years.'

'He'll probably drop in some day and you won't be able to get him to stop talking ... I know you wanted some stories for your article but why don't you do one on ghosts? It's almost Hallowe'en. Mrs McGinley was in this morning and my hair was standing on end with all her stories of headless horsemen and moving lights and clanking chains.

'Everyone seems to be talking about ghosts,' laughed Brian. He told them about the essay and they were both very pleased. Sheila in particular was light-headed with relief. The old Brian was back again.

Brian decided to to to bed early. As he undressed he thought about Barney. Privately, he thought that Barney just hadn't wanted to see Ian and had left as soon as he could decently get away. But why? Maybe he didn't like Ian. Grown-ups could be as difficult as teenagers and he knew he himself had been difficult lately. He also thought about David and Kieran. Well, he just wouldn't let them annoy him. Before he got into bed he looked out of the window. The moon, a little more than a crescent tonight, now seemed warm and friendly, throwing long shadows across the garden, silhouetting the tall trees in the distance with their canopies of leaves. Some animal – a fox? – emerged into the light for a moment, then disappeared.

He quickly fell into a deep untroubled sleep. His nightmare did not haunt him that night.

Brian was up first and had the cereal bowls on the table and was making toast when the rest of the family arrived.

'Don't forget you owe us a turn at the wash-up as well,' Cliona said to her brother with a grin as she sat down to her cereal.

'You don't give up do you,' he laughed.

Breakfast was a noisy meal and Sheila had to remind them a couple of times that it was getting late.

When they were getting their school-bags Sheila said to Ian, 'Did you say you're calling to see Mr. Cassidy today?'

'Yes, this afternoon. He's been in Dublin this past few days. I'll have to put a squib under him. I know solicitors are slow but it's about time everything was fixed up. Jack says he can't understand why it's taking so long.'

As she poured herself another cup of tea when the family had left, Sheila suddenly thought to herself, 'Why waste such a lovely morning doing housework? I'll go for a walk.' Grabbing a sketch-pad and pencils, she put on a warmer jumper and went out into the sunny October morning.

She went through a wooden gate at the back of the

house, and following a rough track through the fields she soon reached the spot she wanted. The oak and hazel wood across the river still had splendid colour, and with the different sized stumps and the hanging twisted branches it made an interesting study. Soon Sheila was busily sketching, housework completely forgotten for the time being.

Brian walked home from school with Michael that evening. Laura was some distance ahead with another girl. Later, as he was sitting at the kitchen table doing his homework, staring out of the window every now and again for inspiration, he was surprised to see the Dohertys arrive.

'I didn't expect to see you so soon again,' he said with a smile when they came into the kitchen.

They were carrying a box which they carefully placed on the floor, and opening it Laura gently removed a lovely young brown water-spaniel.

'Is he for me?' Brian asked in delighted surprise.

'Yes, we thought you would like one,' Laura said, 'Tara had pups and there was only one that had not been booked so we decided you should have him. I hope your parents won't object.'

'They won't! Thanks. He's terrific,' Brian said gratefully, stroking the soft curly coat of the water-spaniel.

'What do you think of him, Dad?' he asked eagerly when Ian came into the kitchen.

'Very nice,' Ian said in an abstracted manner as he walked by, with barely a glance at the dog, calling to his wife, 'Sheila, can you come here for a minute?'

There was a note of urgency in his voice that made Brian pause. Placing the dog back into the box he said good-bye to Laura and Michael and followed Sheila and Ian to the study.

The door was slightly open, and he was about to go into the room when he heard Ian say apologetically, 'I'm sorry, Sheila, but there it is. The land certificate is missing and Mr Cassidy is baffled. It was his father who used to deal with Peter's affairs, but he's been dead for years – anyway I gather he was not the most organised of individuals. Francis Cassidy says it must be somewhere. But it can't be located. It seems that the last registered owner of the property, before Peter came to live here, was a Mr Byrne – he was a cattle-dealer in Letterkenny. Now his nephew is disputing the ownership. Says Peter didn't own Fernhill and had no right to leave it to us.'

'Ian, this is a dreadful shock. I can hardly believe it.' Sheila's normally low-pitched voice had risen in anguish. 'What on earth are we going to do? Will we have to leave the house?'

'It probably won't come to that. The certificate may turn

up. And the sale to Peter must have been registered ... But there's another worrying aspect. Mr Cassidy thinks the claim may be an attempt to make us pay money. If we pay up, the nephew will drop it.'

'How much?'

'Some thousands.'

'Thousands! Where on earth would we get that kind of money in a hurry? To buy something we own.'

'It just might be worth it. Going to law is always a gamble. And we have the money from the sale of the house in Dublin.'

'But we had that earmarked for college and all sorts of things.'

'I know ... but, Sheila, you mustn't worry. Things have to turn out all right. Peter *must* have owned Fernhill. I think the nephew is just chancing his arm.'

'Leave Fernhill?' The words echoed in Brian's head as he turned away from the study door. He hadn't wanted to come here in the first place, and now that he was getting used to the idea they were going to be thrown out. Or have to pay out thousands. Why hadn't his parents gone into the matter thoroughly before they moved, instead of leaving everything to a bumbling old solicitor who didn't seem to know what he was doing?

Brian felt a deep anger building up inside him. He was particularly furious with his father, who was always telling other people where they had gone wrong. And now this! Slowly he went back to the kitchen and the water-spaniel. He'd have to find it a larger box and decide where it was to sleep.

3
Ashbrook

Brian's nightmare returned that night, and he lay staring into the darkness for a long time before sleep came again, but it was a restless sleep and he was dull-eyed and irritable in the morning going out to school.

It was raining at lunch-time so they had to eat in school. Brian, still in a bad mood – he had been unable to concentrate in class all morning – was sitting in the canteen, morosely eating a sandwich, when he saw Kieran and David coming towards him. His suspicions were aroused; it was unlike them to seek him out. He made no objection when they asked to sit down, but he was glad when Michael arrived.

When Kieran had finished his sandwich he nudged David and said, 'Go on then, ask him.'

'Ask who, what?' said Michael with a grin.

'We think Brian should spend a couple of hours in Susannah Parry's house. In Ashbrook,' answered David with a mischievous smile.

'Oh, no, I don't think that's such a good idea,' Michael demurred.

'Why not? If Brian believes in ghosts, here's his chance to meet a real one. He isn't afraid,' argued David.

'Well, you wouldn't stay there on your own,' countered Michael.

'Is this the house you were talking about the other day? Where is it anyway?' Brian wanted to know.

'It's the old house in the trees, a couple of fields away from yours. It's supposed to be haunted. The people who lived there were cousins of ours – they'd be related to you too, in some way,' explained Michael.

'I heard that it's only supposed to be haunted during October,' David chimed in. 'By Susannah Parry,' he added in a low voice.

'The house has been empty for years and years. Nobody ever wants to talk about the place. There was some mention about Susannah Parry having a son who disappeared. But it was all so long ago,' explained Michael.

'Well, what do you say, Brian? How would you like to spend a couple of hours there?' Kieran asked eagerly.

'Why a couple of hours?'

'Because the last fellow who went there only stayed an hour. You would need to do better than that.'

Brian sat in silence for a moment looking at the two boys. Kieran's red hair hung over his eyes, and David's blond hair was dishevelled, because he ran his hands through it continually when he was excited about something.

'I think I'm going to have to show these two they can't push me around,' Brian thought.

'Maybe he is afraid after all,' taunted David.

'Of course I'm not afraid, but Mum and Dad may wonder where I am. I'll do it tomorrow.'

'Why not this evening, before you have time to change your mind,' said David.

'But I've got swimming.'

'Just skip it, and then go home at the usual time.' It

occurred to him that David and Kieran had it all worked out.

'Right, you're on,' he said after a slight hesitation.

'We'll see you safely to the house,' David volunteered.

'Yes,' Kieran agreed, adding, 'Remember you must go into every room and stay at least two hours.'

'And if the ghost of Susannah Parry shows, you'll take back what you said about people in the country. If she doesn't, we'll admit it's only superstition. Right?'

The two boys grinned triumphantly at each other.

Michael was now sitting slightly apart from the others, not wanting to become involved, but Brian felt in control of the situation. He was sure they had a surprise planned for him but he would turn the tables on them. Missing swimming for one day was not going to hurt. Anyway, he really didn't feel up to the fifteen-mile bus trip to the swimming-pool this evening. He felt he didn't want to talk to anyone.

When school was ended for the day the boys met at the gates as arranged. They went quickly through the town and soon they were passing the old Catholic church and walking at a good pace out along Forest Road.

'Are you sure you want to do this?' Michael asked Brian in a whisper when they had left the town far behind them.

'Yes, why not.' Brian was still in a grimly determined frame of mind. 'If I don't do it now David and Kieran will think it's because I'm afraid.'

'It will be dark in an hour or so. How will you find your way home?' asked Michael worriedly.

'I've got my torch in my bag. I need it when I get off the bus. You know what the lane to our house is like.'

'Well, it's not as long or as twisted as Parry's lane,' said Kieran darkly, overhearing the last remark, and a short time later when they turned into a rutted narrow laneway Brian understood exactly what he meant.

'Oh, no, I think Mrs Clarke has seen us,' Kieran muttered as they were passing a small cottage with a neat front garden.

'Where is she?' asked Michael in a low voice.

'There, at the side of the house, feeding the hens.'

'Just wave. And for goodness sake don't run, or she will wonder what we're up to,' said David.

Mrs Clarke waved to the boys, and Kieran and David waved back. They walked on, two on either side of the high ridge of grass that grew in the centre of the lane, avoiding the brambles that snaked across their path. There was silence until Kieran spoke loudly to David. 'I think he looks scared.'

'Maybe he wants to turn back,' said David jeeringly.

'I'm not scared, and I don't want to turn back,' replied Brian shortly. In the distance across the fields, he could see the chimneys of Fernhill. He wished he were home again.

Kieran pointed off to his left and said, 'Brian could always take the short way home.'

'He's better going by the road. At least he will know where he is then,' said Michael firmly.

'All right, all right. It was just a suggestion.'

'And not a very good one, like most of your suggestions.' Michael sounded on edge.

By this time they were passing a high hawthorn hedge on their left, and as they rounded yet another bend and passed a group of ancient sycamore and horse-chestnut-trees, the house came into full view.

'There you are. Ashbrook at last,' announced David.

It was a large, two-storied, slated house of dull grey stone, with a square porch in front. Some of the panes in the windows on the ground floor were broken and had been replaced by rough boards. Having made their way up the overgrown avenue, they paused before going up the stone steps to the porch. Looking up, Brian suddenly shivered. For a fleeting moment he though he had seen a face at one of the upstairs windows. He quickly turned his head, but when he looked back again, there was nothing. Just a blank, staring void.

'Was there someone there?' he wondered uneasily as he took stock of his surroundings.

Once there would have been a gravelled sweep in front of the house. Now the grass grew right up to the bottom step, and there were small tufts growing here and there through cracks in the stone. To his right, he could see old ivy-covered walls, either tumbling down or completely flattened in places – maybe they had once sheltered a well-tended garden. Just beyond the walls, four twisted and broken apple-trees, their trunks encased in choking brambles, starkly revealed what was left of the orchard. To his left were three single-storied outbuildings with corrugated zinc roofs, which were either rusting or had large gaping holes; on one, a sheet of zinc hung listlessly from a single nail, moving only when there was a sudden gust of wind.

'You have to lift the door.' David's voice made him jump. 'It sticks.' Pulling away a flat piece of wood that was nailed in front of the lock, he deftly inserted his hand through a crack and released the catch.

'How do we know he won't just leave after we're gone?' Kieran asked suspiciously.

'I said I'd stay didn't I,' said Brian indignantly.

'You can trust him,' said Michael loyally.

'Just remember, you must stay two hours and go into each room,' instructed David.

Grasping the large black knocker and knob, Brian lifted the door and with his shoulder he pushed at the same time. It reluctantly moved inwards allowing him enough room to enter, and with a thumbs-up sign, the others went off down the lane again.

Opening the glass-panelled inner door, he found himself in a large tiled hall, facing a beautifully carved staircase which led to the next floor. When he closed the door, he was surprised to see dusty umbrella and walking-stick handles emerging from a tall wooden stand in the corner. Somehow he had expected the place to be completely empty.

There was a door on his left and, opening it, Brian found himself in the dusty interior of what used to be the kitchen. There was a smaller room off that which was lined with shelves. A rusting tin-opener lay beside a soup-plate on the narrow window-sill. Taking a closer look he saw small heaps of chewed paper in the corners of the shelves. 'Probably mice,' he thought, and then, with a shiver of distaste, he wondered if it could have been rats.

A thick layer of dust covered everything but the place was not that untidy. An open drawer in one of the units revealed a few forks and spoons, and the presses were empty except for two pale-blue cracked cups. The oven door of an old black Stanley range lay wide open and there were large brown patches on the wall above, where chimney soot had dripped unheeded for years.

Cobwebs draped the windows, together with what was left of the net curtains, which may once have been pristine white but were now a limp mixture of brown and yellow, riddled throughout with holes. Looking at them he was amazed that they hung together.at all.

As he looked at the kitchen table with a few chairs haphazardly grouped around it, Brian felt the first stirrings of curiosity as he wondered about Susannah Parry and her son.

He moved quickly across the wide hall, his feet crunching the lime plaster that had fallen from the wall here and there, leaving ugly gaping holes, and opening another door he found himself in the drawing-room. It was a large square room and the bare floor-boards were hidden under a thick coating of dust. The two windows were partially covered by long tattered green velvet curtains, which must once have looked elegant, but now gave the room a sad depressing air. The mottled mirror which hung above the black fireplace did nothing to dispel the air of gloom. Here and there small patches of striped wallpaper clung stubbornly to damp walls, and again he noticed the small heaps of chewed paper around the skirting-boards.

He went into the next room, which was smaller and without furniture. 'Probably the dining-room,' he thought as he surveyed the long narrow room which was dimly lit by one tall window. Also downstairs was a small toilet with a cracked porcelain wash-basin, where the constant drip from one of the taps had left long blue and brown streaks, and a cloakroom, bare except for the large curved coat-hooks.

Closing the creaking door as quietly as possible he came back to the hall again. As he grasped the dark mahogany handrail at the bottom of the stairs, he hesitated. A sudden, unwelcome thought had struck him. What if he had really seen someone at the window. Could there be someone upstairs in one of the bedrooms, waiting for him.' He laughed shakily to himself and thought, 'Wouldn't David and Kieran love to see me now, scared and uncertain, afraid to go upstairs.'

Taking a firmer hold of the handrail he slowly made his way up the carpetless stairs. Some of the steps creaked loudly, others gave no more than a faint groan as he moved upwards.

There were two doors at the top of the stairs, and opening the first one he found himself in a large L-shaped room. In the corner facing him, a single iron bed stood lopsidedly on the bare floor. Moving further into the room he could see a castor lying in front of the boarded-up fire-place, where soot still seeped on to the floor, creating a large dark stain.' Like the map of Africa,' he thought. There was an old wardrobe in one corner, and an arm-chair, covered in dark brown material, was pushed up against the gable wall.

Around the corner from the fireplace, he was surprised to see another door. This led into a small room with a window looking out over the porch. Book shelves lined one wall, and a low chair stood in a corner. 'Must have been a study,' he decided as he moved back through the L-shaped room again.

The next door opened into a long narrow bathroom. It had a tall sash window with stained-glass side-panes of red and blue.

He was passing the tall grimy window that lighted the wide landing when he stopped suddenly. On the wall of an alcove facing him was an African mask. The raffia fringe

looked like real hair and the thick lips were parted. And as he stood there looking he was sure the expression on the face changed to a menacing smile.

Something was tugging at his memory, but it took him a moment to fully absorb what he had seen and then it hit him.

There was no doubt about it. That was the detail from his nightmare that kept eluding him – the African mask. Its sinister face was as real to him as the staircase down which, in his dreams, he had struggled so vainly. It, too, was the same. Somehow he was reliving his nightmare. What could it possibly mean?

Trying to stay calm he thought of his promise to visit each room, so averting his gaze from the mask, he hurriedly looked into the darkening interiors.

The first two, with windows in the north-facing wall, had a fine view of the oakwoods, and he could clearly see the river, and the narrow wooden footbridge which spanned the stream that fed it.

A damp smell pervaded the air and there were large spots of mildew on the walls. The only furniture was a light wickerwork chair, which stood beside the fireplace, in one, and a small circular mirror in the other.

When he came to the third door there was a slight tremor in his sweating hand as he slowly turned the knob. He thought again of the face at the window, It must have been in this room, which overlooked the neglected garden.

A sigh of relief escaped through his dry lips when he saw that there was nobody there and he thought with a little laugh, 'I really must be careful and not get carried away.' Just because he'd been told the house was haunted, he'd begun seeing things. There were no such things as ghosts.

It was, as he had said, silly superstition. People who

were easily frightened invented stories about hauntings and ghosts and came to believe in them. It was funny about the African mask, though. Still, that was probably just a coincidence.

His confidence had returned again, but he had still some time to wait before he could go home. He'd have to decide where to wait.

Downstairs, the glass-panelled door rattled continuously, and he made up his mind. He'd wait upstairs. At least it was not quite as dismal as downstairs, although some of the rooms were damp and he did not feel comfortable in them. He had liked the small study off the L-shaped room and as it was drier and warmer than the others, he decided to stay there. He did not pause to look at the African mask again as he passed by, but went straight to the L-shaped room. Again, he noticed the heaps of chewed paper, and here and there he could still see a large flower or green stem of the patterned wallpaper that once hung upon the walls. He closed the wardrobe door and a few empty coat-hangers rattled loudly. There was a thick coating of grime on the window and he wiped clean a small circle. Through it he could see the twisting laneway and fields, and the large tracts of bogland in the distance. Even the gable of Mrs Clarke's cottage was visible through the trees.

As he sat on the window-ledge looking out, something caught his eye, and rubbing a corner of the window-board he could see, carved deeply into the wood, the letters R.I.P. And underneath that were the letters R.G. which were much larger.

Who had carved the letters and what did they mean? he wondered as he moved into the study.

From the window there he could see the neglected garden and crumbling walls and, in the distance, the main road with the odd car speeding by. It was oddly comforting.

He was beginning to feel thirsty. Luckily he always brought food and drink along to eat on the bus after swimming, and as he fumbled in his school-bag for a can of coke he realised that the room was almost in complete darkness now. He wasn't feeling very hungry this evening, but when half his coke had gone, he decided to eat his bag of crisps.

As he sat there in the corner, he found himself wondering again about Susannah Parry. Who was she? Had she lived in Ashbrook when it was still beautiful. And what was the mystery about her and her son? Old Barney Flood would probably know. He'd have to ask him about her.

The silence around him was broken only by the munching of the crisps, so at first Brian was unsure if he had heard a noise or not. He stopped eating for a moment, the crisps softening in his mouth as he listened attentively.

Yes, there it was again! it sounded like a loud creak from the stairway. The crisps slid down his throat and he sat tensely, his eyes fastened on the doorway. He swallowed dryly when he heard his name being said. In a whisper at first he heard, 'Brian,' and then louder it came. 'Are you there, Brian?'

4

The Moving Light

Jumping up he almost upset his coke as he ran through the doorway and into the L-shaped room.

'Laura? Cliona? What on earth are you two doing here?' he asked in relieved surprise.

'I met Laura and Michael and they told me where you were,' explained Cliona. 'Then I remembered you didn't take your jacket to school with you today so I decided to bring it across to you, and Laura offered to show me the short way.'

'Well, thanks. I was beginning to find it rather cold here,' he said pulling on the jacket. He hated wearing it to school because of the hassle trying to find it in the cloak-room later.

'Michael told me about the dare,' said Cliona 'He's worried about you being here on your own. Why don't you come on home with us now?'

'You've proved that you're not afraid to stay in this house.' Laura smiled at him.

'No, I must stay another hour,' explained Brian. 'I have a feeling David and Kieran will come and try to frighten me now that it's almost dark.'

'That would be just like them. Pair of twits.'

'Do you know anything about Susannah Parry?' Brian asked her.

'Not very much. There was always this story about Ash-brook being haunted. It seems Susannah Parry's son disappeared years ago and she used to go out at night searching for him. And sometimes kids would say they saw lights in the windows.'

'Well, they'll see lights tonight anyway,' said Brian, switching on his torch for a little while.

'Now we must go,' said Laura. 'I've some homework to do before I come over to babysit Paul.'

Brian had forgotten that Ian and Sheila were going to Sligo to see Brian Friel's *Dancing at Lughnasa*, which was playing at the Hawks Well theatre. They were both looking forward to seeing it.

'Will I come downstairs with you?' Brian offered.

'No, we'll be all right, Brian,' Laura assured him. 'We'll see you later.'

He stood for a moment or two watching them go down to the hall, and when the sound of their footsteps had faded he thought how silent it all was. He was grateful for the warmth of his jacket, and he was touched that Cliona had thought of bringing it to him. Laura, too. He felt that she and Michael were going to become good friends.

After the girls had gone, he felt himself getting more restless, wishing the time was up.

At first the silence was broken only by the sound of his impatient footsteps as he prowled from one window to the other. He could not distinguish the shapes of the cars any more, but he could see the headlights disappearing around a curve in the road to reappear on the straight again. Now the surrounding hillside began to be dotted with the lights of scattered houses. Everyone was safely at home.

The wind had risen and he could hear the sheet of corrugated zinc crash loudly as it rose and fell against the outhouse wall. Then he heard a tapping noise on the roof of the house. He realised almost immediately that it was a branch of one of the large sycamore trees at the side of the house, swaying in the wind and touching the slates. And every now and then there was a slithering sound as a broken twig careered down the roof and into the guttering. A few moments later the whole process would start all over again. It was beginning to get on his nerves. He would be glad when it was time to go home.

Tired of wandering aimlessly between the two rooms, he threw himself into the brown armchair in the L-shaped room. He was immediately enveloped in a cloud of dust which made him sneeze, and a broken spring dug viciously into his side. He was pushing it down into the bowels of the chair when his hand felt a smallish hard object. It felt like a book. The room was now in complete darkness, so he switched on his torch to see. It was a book, a diary. Dark blue, with most of the gold lettering missing from the cover.

'Great,' he thought, 'this will make the last fifteen minutes fly.'

He had just opened it when a small sound make him sit up alertly. If the wind had not died down he probably would not have heard it. There it was again, a stealthy rustle, coming from the direction of the stairs. He quickly stuck the diary into his inside pocket and shielded the light from his torch with his left hand. He had been expecting something like this to happen. It was unlikely that Kieran and David would let a chance like this pass. They were coming to frighten him.

He crossed the room to the fireplace, his Doc boots making little noise. Silently he moved along the wall until he was behind the half-door, and there he stopped. He would be ready for them. Switching off the torch he waited.

Through the gap between the door and door frame could see the beam of light coming up the stairs. It was very bright, and he grinned to himself and thought, 'They're probably more frightened than I am. They must have taken the most powerful torch they could find.'

But they were slow in coming. He was beginning to get impatient and was tempted to call out, when at last he saw the light coming around the door.

Getting ready to pounce, he suddenly pulled back in consternation. There was nobody there. The light was moving on its own! There was a blue haze around it, and he watched in disbelief as it moved jerkily across the room to the bed in the corner.

The room had suddenly grown very cold. A deep chill seemed to penetrate his whole body, but, strangely, beads of perspiration bubbled on his forehead.

Then the light grew dimmer, and started to change shape, lengthening, and blurring at the edges.

And then came a sigh, a low plaintive sound at first, which became louder, until it filled the room. And staring about him in terror, it seemed to Brian as if the very walls were moving.

His torch slipped from his icy nerveless fingers, his heart was pounding madly, and before he slid down the wall in a deep faint he was thinking in desperation, 'I must get to the stairs.'

5

Return of a Stranger

Meanwhile, at Fernhill, the others were getting worried.

'Laura, Brian should have been home by now,' Cliona said anxiously. 'Should we ring Michael and ask him to go and see what's keeping him?'

'Michael's not at home. He's playing table-tennis to-night. Let's leave it another little while. I'm sure he's all right.' But she too was worried. She had put on the outside light as she had been expecting him some time ago.

Quietly opening the front door she stood looking into the night, wondering what to do next, when a movement at the side of the house made her jump. Someone was coming towards the door.

'Brian, it's you! We were getting worried about you. But what on earth are you doing out here? And look at your clothes, they're filthy. And you're breathless.'

Brian looked at her strangely. 'Who are you?'

'You must be joking!' laughed Laura. 'I saw you about an hour ago. Cliona and I brought you your jacket. Remember?'

As Brian continued to look at her with a tense look, she continued, 'I'm Laura, Michael's sister. Michael – he's in your class.'

'Michael? I know nobody called Michael.' He looked around him. 'I came the short way, I think there's someone chasing me. I want to get home.'

'But, Brian, you *are* home.'

'Why do you call me Brian? My name is Richard... I'm looking for Fernhill.'

'This *is* Fernhill.'

'How could it be? It's all so changed There isn't a porch and that gate shouldn't be here.' His voice trailed away as he looked around him in bewilderment.

'If this...' began Laura. She had been about to say, 'If this is your idea of a joke it isn't funny,' but the look on his face made her stop. This was no joke. There was definitely something wrong. Maybe he had fallen. That would explain his dishevelled appearance.

'Come on, you're all mixed up,' she said soothingly, leading the way into the house. 'You'll feel better when you sit down for a while.'

'Brian! There you are!' Cliona and Niamh jumped up when they came into the kitchen.

The bewildered look came back.

'I told this girl already, my name is Richard. Who are you two?'

'Brian, that's not funny. We were worried about you,' said Cliona, looking at Laura for support.

'He didn't recognise me either. He seems to have lost his memory. I think he should lie down, and I'd better ring Doctor Boyle. I'm sure he'll be all right.'

'We'll help Brian upstairs, while you ring the doctor,' said Cliona. He offered no resistance. Just closed his eyes and allowed himself to be guided upstairs. They did not have to wait long until the doctor arrived and, after examining Brian, he spoke to Laura first. 'He's still confused and a bit drowsy, he probably had a fall and may be concussed. To be on the safe side I'll have him admitted to Sligo General for observation.'

'But how will we get him there. Ian and Sheila are at the theatre in Sligo tonight,' explained Laura.

'I can take him. I'm going there anyway in a little while. I'll ring Casualty to expect us, and you could ring the theatre and leave a message for Ian and Sheila to contact the hospital. Don't alarm them.'

'Easier said than done,' thought Laura, but when she got through to Sheila she was able to assure them that Dr Boyle had said that there was nothing wrong physically, and that bringing him to Sligo for observation was merely being extra careful. She said nothing about Brian saying his name was Richard. Maybe that phase of whatever he was suffering from would have disappeared by the time Ian and Sheila got to the hospital.

After Dr Boyle left with Brian, Cliona and Niamh sat with Laura in the kitchen, but none of them was able to concentrate on television, so after reassuring the girls again that Brian was in good hands and would be okay, she persuaded them to go to bed.

She tried to read but the words were a jumble on the page in front of her, so instead she listened to music on the radio as the hours dragged by. She had been dozing off when the sound of a car made her sit up, and going to the window she saw that Sheila and Ian had returned.

'How is he?' she asked anxiously when they came into the kitchen.

'Well, his X-rays and brian scan are normal, but he's very confused. Says his name is Richard. I would have liked to ask him more about it but we were told not to let him talk too much. They think he may have fallen and hit his head. He's in a darkened room and the doctors want him kept quiet for now. But we're hoping he'll get home tomorrow,' Sheila explained, adding, 'And thanks for your help, Laura. You were great, you must be tired. Ian will run you home.'

In the morning Sheila rang the hospital, and was told that Brian had had a comfortable night and would be discharged that evening.

But when Ian arrived home with him, the girls were dismayed to hear him still insisting that his name was Richard.

'What is the matter with him?' they asked when he went upstairs.

'Well, the doctors can find nothing wrong physically. No injuries. They think it's possible that he might be suffering from a type of amnesia that is called double personality. That means that not only has he lost his memory, but he has replaced his own identity with another one.'

'How could he have forgotten about Niamh and Paul and me?' Cliona asked incredulously. 'Has he forgotten about moving from Dublin? About coming here?'

'I'm afraid so. He had to be told who we all are.'

'How long will it last?' asked Niamh.

'It could last days or weeks. Nobody can be sure.'

'But how could such a terrible thing happen?'

'The doctors said if he was suffering from great anxiety or stress over a period of time, that could have triggered it. Or possibly some severe emotional shock. Anyway what he needs now is plenty of rest, and we mustn't force him to remember. So we're going to have to be patient, and explain things to him, and hope his memory returns soon.' Ian did his best to sound cheerful'.

'A severe emotional shock? Do you think staying in Ashbrook could have given Brian such a shock?' whispered

Niamh to Cliona.

'No, of course not,' she replied, stoutly with more conviction than she felt.

The kitchen door suddenly burst open and Brian stood there. He stared at them for some moments before saying angrily, 'I want you to know something. My name is Richard Grier. I am *not* Richard Ignatius Parry. Do you understand?' He shouted the last words.

There was stunned silence for a moment, then Sheila said calmly, 'We're trying to understand, but this is all very difficult for us too. And I think the best thing we can do is follow the doctors' instructions, so you should go to bed and rest now. Come.'

Her soothing voice had an immediate effect. Brian allowed her to take his arm without protest and Ian followed as they went upstairs.

'Who is Richard Grier? Why should he say his name is not Richard Ignatius Parry?' Niamh said to Cliona when they were alone.

'It must be something to do with staying in Ashbrook. The name Parry must have stuck in his mind. But I don't know where he got Richard Grier from.'

'Do you think we should tell Mum and Dad about Ashbrook?'

'I don't know. I wish Laura was at home. I'd like to talk to her first. But they won't be back until late tonight. We'll leave it for now, and go over and see her in the morning.'

The girls were up early next morning. There had been a slight drizzle but by the time they were ready to set off for Laura's house it was dry and sunny again. They ran most of the way, and when they arrived, Paula smiled and remarked how the country air was bringing colour to their cheeks. Laura and Michael were only finishing their breakfast so the girls joined them in the kitchen. Cliona explained what the doctors had said about Brian's condition.

'But then, last night, he got violent, insisting that his name was Richard Grier, and not Richard Ignatius Parry,' said Niamh.

'Up to that he only said his name was Richard,' added Cliona.

'So that's what the letters R.I.P. stand for. They're carved on the window-sill, in the L shaped room in Parry's house,' said Michael slowly

'Did anyone tell Brian what they meant?' asked Laura.

'No, I'm sure David and Kieran didn't know, and I certainly didn't. We had all seen them, but we thought it meant Rest in Peace. And we'd often wondered about R.G. which is carved in much bigger letters beneath R.I.P.'

'Brian never mentioned the letters when we were there. I wonder did he see them?' said Cliona.

'He had such an odd stare when he said his name was Richard Grier, not Parry. He shouted it. Do you think something awful happened to him after you two left?' asked Niamh.

Nobody, answered, until Cliona finally said, 'What do you think we should do, Laura?'

'You're going to have to tell Ian and Sheila about Brian's visit to Ashbrook,' she replied.

Cliona and Niamh exchanged worried looks, and they both said, 'They're not going to like it.'

'I know, but they must be told now,' said Laura firmly.

'We shouldn't have let him go there alone,' groaned Michael.

'Don't blame yourself. He was fine when we left him,' Cliona said comfortingly. 'Come on, Niamh. We'd better go home and explain.'

'Dad will go off his head,' said Niamh as they hurried along the road.

'No he won't, he'll understand.' Cliona crossed her fingers behind her back.

6
Remembering Times Past

Sheila and Ian were in the kitchen talking quietly when the girls returned. There was no sign of Brian or Paul.

Taking a deep breath, Cliona launched into the story of Brian's visit to Ashbrook. Ian's colour deepened and he threw his hands in the air when she had finished. In the ensuing silence, Niamh whispered to her sister in a smug voice, 'There, what did I tell you? I said he'd go off his head.'

'Oh, shut up,' said Cliona through clenched teeth, and when she saw her sister's face begin to melt, she warned, 'Don't dare cry.'

But the expected explosion from Ian never happened, He just looked increasingly worried as he said to Sheila, 'Something must have happened to him there.'

'What could have happened? You don't believe it was a ghost, do you? Unless . . .,' her voice faltered a little, '. . . a tramp broke in and gave him a fright.'

They were interrupted by a gentle tap on the kitchen door. It was Jack with Laura and Michael.

'I rang Paula this morning about Brian. Did she tell you what the doctors said?' Sheila asked Jack when he sat down.

'About the amnesia? Yes, I'm sorry to hear about it. I hope it won't last long,' he said, adding, 'Laura and

Michael have been telling me about the visit to the Parry house.'

'I was just thinking about Susannah Parry and her son when you came in. You must remember them, Jack.' said Ian.

'Well, I remember Susannah and I saw Richard a few times. I must admit, I haven't thought about the Parrys in years. I used to hear my father talking about them occasionally. Generally people didn't – I'm not sure why.'

'But if Brian thinks he's Richard Parry, why would he come back to this house?' asked Laura. 'He said he was coming home. But his home was Ashbrook.'

'Did you know that Susannah and Richard lived in this house for a while?' Jack asked.

'No, I never knew that.' Ian was startled.

'Anyway, what Brian actually said was that his name was Richard Grier, and he was not Richard Ignatius Parry.' Sheila reminded them.

'Did he say that?' Now Jack looked worried.

'I asked Barney Flood this morning when I met him on the road if he knew anyone called Grier and he said the name meant nothing to him. Why, is it important?' asked Laura.

'It was the name of Susannah's first husband. He was Richard's father. When he died she became ill. She had no really close relations, there were only distant cousins like us. Anyway, Ian's grand-uncle, Peter, and his mother brought her and Richard here to live,' explained Jack.

'Where do the Parrys come into the story'?

'Susannah had been widowed for a couple of years when she met Albert Parry. He had lived in South Africa for years, working in Kimberly, in the diamond fields. He was supposed to have made a lot of money when he was still quite a young man, and he came here and bought Ashbrook. It seems he never mixed much, preferring his own company, so people around here didn't bother him. Though there were a few people grateful to him. Some of the locals were interested in working in the diamond fields and he helped them to get work. Barney Flood was one of them, used to work with him on and off for years.

'Parry lived a solitary life. No close friends. So it came as a shock when he decided to get married – and even more of a shock when Susannah accepted him.'

'What happened after Susannah and Albert had got married?' Niamh asked.

'She and Richard went to live at Ashbrook, and for a time it seemed that Albert was becoming more sociable. He would take Susannah and Richard into Rossmore on a Saturday for shopping, and sometimes he would visit the neighbours with them. Richard and Susannah used to love visiting your grand-uncle, Ian.'

'Was Richard happy? Did he have friends?' Michael wanted to know.

Jack hesitated a little while before replying. 'No, I don't think he had any friends, other than his mother. She stopped sending him to school. Said it was because he was delicate, and she would educate him at home herself. And then they said they didn't want any of the neighbouring children visiting the house. And soon after that Susannah stopped visiting, even to Peter's. Sometimes they were seen in Donegal town, or Letterkenny. People would have liked to remain friendly with Susannah and Richard, but Albert was a dour man, didn't want people around, so they left them alone.'

Sheila sat quite still, deep in thought, remembering the day they had moved into this house. Little had she realised then, just a few short months ago, that their lives would change so much, and that because of Brian they would become so involved in the history of Susannah Parry.

'What happened to them, the Parrys?' asked Cliona.

'We had moved to Australia at that stage. We must have been there about a year when my father got a letter telling him that Richard had disappeared. Just ran away I expect. He can't have been very happy . . . Then there was another letter, telling him Albert Parry had gone back to Africa. And someone wrote to him when Susannah died. And each letter started all the talk about the family again. I'm sorry now I didn't pay more attention at the time. But I was very young then and it was all so far away . . . But Ian, you must remember something about the Parrys?'

'When I first came to grand-uncle Peter's on holiday, I was very curious about Ashbrook,' said Ian slowly. 'But he never wanted to talk about the place. All he would say when I asked was, "It's just an old house. Leave it be." I never knew Susannah, of course. Or Richard.'

'I remember my father telling me how very fond of Susannah and Richard, Peter was – he was totally against the marriage to Albert. And when they stopped visiting him, he blamed it on Albert's influence on Susannah . . . . And now I must be off. But before I go, I think Michael has something to say to you and Sheila.'

'Yes,' stammered Michael. 'I'm sorry we let Brian go to the Parry house on his own.'

'Never mind that now,' Ian said, not unkindly, 'but, tell me, which of you told him about Richard Ignatius Parry and Richard Grier?'

'We didn't tell him. None of us knew the names,' protested Michael. We had seen the letters R.I.P. carved on the window-sill. But we always thought it meant Rest In

Peace. And we never knew what R.G. stood for. Honestly.'

'I told Brian that Susannah Parry had a son who had disappeared, but that was all I knew. I never heard his name before this either,' said Laura.

'Well, someone must have told him about it,' insisted Ian.

'He knew nothing about Ashbrook or the Parry family until we told him at school,' said Michael firmly.

'All he told me on Friday night was that his name was Richard, that he thought someone was chasing him and he had taken the short way home,' said Laura wrinkling her brow, trying to remember. 'Oh, and he said that Fernhill was his home and that it was all changed.'

'Brian doesn't know the short way from Ashbrook,' said Michael.

'Someone must have shown him. It's the only explanation, isn't it?' Ian sounded puzzled.

'It's a bit of a mystery at the moment but I'm sure there is some logical explanation,' said Jack as he left.

When Ian and Sheila went indoors again, Paul pestered Michael to play football with him, and as Laura went to the door to watch them, she noticed Brian sitting dejectedly on the stairs, stroking the dog.

Going over to him, she asked, 'How are you feeling today?'

'I'm all right I suppose. I've been told it was you who gave me Samson here. Thanks, Laura. He's a lovely dog.'

'You're welcome, Brian. I can see Samson likes you.'

'You know it feels funny hearing my name. The doctors say I have amnesia and that even though I think of myself as Richard, my name is really Brian Cooper. Even though Sheila and Ian are very nice, and I like Cliona and Niamh and Paul, it's all rather weird. It's strange that I don't remember anything about our life together at all. It seems we lived in Dublin before moving here. But I feel as if I belonged here always.'

'I think you're going to love living here, and I'm sure your memory will come back soon, Brian. Just give it time,' said Laura, adding, 'I still think you must have fallen at Parry's house.'

'I can't remember a thing about it. And when I try too hard to recall that evening I get a blinding headache. It's so frustrating.' Brian banged his fist on the wall beside him.

'Don't upset yourself like this. Just don't think about that evening at all. Take things as they come and I'm sure your memory will come back . . . It's such a nice day. Why not take Samson outside for a little while?'

'Yes, you're right. I'll do that. There's no point moping about the place.'

Laura went back to the kitchen, where Cliona and Niamh were sitting with their mother.

'I just wish things were back the way they were before,' Cliona said.

'Yes, I know how you feel,' Sheila agreed.

'Do you think Brian is too sick to help me with my Hallowe'en costume this year?' Paul put his head around the door.

'I think it's better to leave him alone for the moment. He needs peace and quiet just now. Maybe Cliona and Niamh could help you. There are plenty of old clothes in those two trunks in the attic,' said Sheila with a smile.

'Great!'

'Laura, you have good ideas, could you stay for another while and help?' asked Cliona.

Laura agreed willingly and laughing they ran off, pulling Paul after them, their troubles momentarily forgotten.

Later Sheila took a plate of shortbread to the children in the attic. They were all sitting on the floor, the colourful contents of the two trunks spilling out around them. 'This will be your first Hallowe'en party in the parish hall,' Laura was saying. 'I hope Brian will come too. There are plenty of old black clothes that would make terrific capes. And there's a great selection of masks in Coyle's shop in Rossmore.'

As she handed around the shortbread, it struck Sheila that attics and trunks were always possible hiding-places for missing documents. In stories. Could it happen in real life?

'What are you doing?' Laura asked when Sheila started rummaging through the trunks, scattering the remaining

clothes on to the floor.

'It just occurred to me that a very important document, which is missing, could have been put into one of the trunks. We've searched but maybe not well enough.'

When she drew a blank, Niamh said, 'Could it be in there?' pointing at two wobbly dressing-tables with their drawers hanging open.

'I'll take a look there too,' said Sheila, but again she was disappointed.

'Why is it so important?' Cliona asked.

'It's the land certificate which will show that Peter bought Fernhill from Mr Byrne. We need it to prove that it belongs to us. The nephew of the previous owner is now saying that he owns Fernhill. That it was never sold to Peter and that it was not his to give us.'

'What if you can't find it? Does it mean we'd have to leave?' Cliona asked in dismay.

'I'm sure it won't come to that. There are other ways of proving ownership.' Sheila hoped she sounded convincing.

'We love it at Fernhill, we can't leave. We must find this land certificate.' Niamh's voice was determined.

'But how?' Sheila was thinking as she made her way downstairs again, leaving the children talking about the possible whereabouts of the vital piece of paper.

'We haven't done much about my costume yet.' Paul interrupted the girls.

'We've plenty of time,' said Laura. 'Anyway, I must go now. I promised to help Mum, and I've been gone hours.'

'If only Brian were his old self again, it would all be fun,' sighed Cliona.

'He will be by then,' Laura said confidently as they left the attic.

7

Simon Harvey: Psychologist

Tea that evening was a quiet meal. Brian was more cheerful later when they sat down to watch telly. He had no memory at all of his favourite programmes and the girls, to tease him, told him that one he had particularly disliked was, in fact, his top choice in the old days. He refused to believe it, and in the ensuing banter and talk, it almost seemed as if he were recovering his memory.

It was bright and sunny next morning, although there was a chill in the air. After a late breakfast Brian put on Samson's lead and took him for a walk. On his way back he met Laura, and they strolled along together.

'Michael is coming over later to see you. He's waiting for Dad to fix his bike,' explained Laura, and then asked, 'Did Cliona and Niamh tell you we're dressing up for the Hallowe'en party in the parish hall?'

'Yes, they were talking about it last night. I probably will go, though I still feel like a stranger. I keep thinking of myself as Richard Grier. We were looking at telly and they tried to convince me that a pretty awful programme was my favourite. I hated it. Then they confessed it was a joke. But what does that prove? Thousands of people must hate that programme. Then they showed me a photograph album and Ian and Sheila kept looking at me so hopefully that somehow I felt I was letting them down, when I didn't recognise anyone. I'm so confused.'

'There's Sheila waving to you from the barn steps,' said Laura as they came closer to the house.

'I promised to help her clear some of the rubbish out of the barn. You know she's into painting and she'd love to turn the barn into a studio. Are you coming to talk to her?' asked Brian when he let Samson off the lead.

Sheila was dressed in an old jumper and jeans and was already putting rubbish into refuse sacks when Laura and Brian came into the barn. Smiling, she handed Brian a sweeping-brush and said, 'Would you like to start in that corner?'

'What can I do?' Laura asked.

'Help me to fill the refuse sacks.'

They worked away from some time, mostly in silence, until Sheila told them to take a break.

'You've done wonders,' she said as she surveyed the barn with satisfaction, but then her smile dimmed and she sighed, 'If only . . .'

'If only you could find the land certificate,' Laura finished the sentence for her.

'Yes, it's on my mind a lot. We have looked everywhere we can possibly think of. And Mr Cassidy has too. But we still can't find it. I'd hate to have to leave Fernhill.'

'Why would you have to leave Fernhill?' asked Brian.

'Of course – you haven't heard . . . The last owner's nephew is saying that this place really belongs to him, that it was never sold to grand-uncle Peter. And we can't prove he's wrong until we find the land certificate. There must be letters from Mr Cassidy's father – he was the solicitor – about the sale of the property, but we can't find those either.'

Brian jumped off the box he had been sitting on, shouting in excitement, 'I know what you're looking for now. They're all together, in a bundle, tied with a piece of string.'

'Brian, you couldn't possibly know where they are,' said Sheila, emphatically at first and then more uncertainly, 'Could you?'

'I could! They're in the attic. Come on, I'll show you,' he said with a laugh.

Sheila and Laura ran out of the barn after Brian and as they went into the house Sheila called out, 'Ian, do come quickly. Brian says the land certificate is in a bundle in the attic.'

'That's impossible. I searched there, and so did you – only yesterday,' he said irritably, but he followed them upstairs anyway.

'Brian says he knows where the land certificate is,' Sheila repeated again to Cliona, Niamh and Paul who had come upstairs to see what the fuss was about.

'Right, where is it then?' asked Ian.

'In there,' Brian said, pointing to the smallest trunk.

'No, it's not there. I searched that trunk thoroughly.' Sheila turned away in disappointment.

'Wait, don't go. Look!' Brian started pulling clothes from the trunk, strewing them chaotically about him.

'There,' he said breathlessly when the last article was discarded. The others stood silently behind him and watched as he pressed a screw in the bracket that held one of the leather handles. There was a collective intake of breath when the false bottom sprang back, to reveal a bundle of papers, neatly tied with narrow string, on the true floor of the trunk.

'Open it quickly,' said Sheila when Brian handed the

bundle to Ian. He examined the papers closely for a moment in silence, and then said with a wide smile, 'I can hardly believe it. This is what we've been looking for all the time. The land certificate. And letters from the solicitor to Peter as well. All the proof we need that Fernhill belongs to us.'

As Cliona and Niamh hugged each other, Laura said, 'And it's all thanks to Brian.'

'Yes, indeed it is. This is such a relief, Brian.'

'But how could you possibly have known where they were,' Ian said, turning to his son.

'Of course I knew where they were. This is where they've always been kept,' Brian said irritably, rubbing his hand across his forehead.

'Are you feeling all right, Brian?' Sheila asked in concern.

'No, I feel rather sick, and I've got a terrible headache. And I told you that my name is Richard.' The last words were said in a loud voice that made the others jump.

'I think you had better lie down for a while. Here, let me help you.' Ian went quickly to his son's side.

And Brian, whose face was pale and shiny with perspiration and whose eyes had now taken on a glazed look, did not speak to Laura and the others, but allowed Ian to lead him gently from the attic.

There was a short silence after Brian had left the attic.

Niamh was the first to speak. 'What can it mean? How could he possibly have known those papers were in the trunk?' There was a tremble in her voice.

'She's right. It wasn't as if he discovered them by accident,' said Laura, adding 'He *knew* they were there. And when he said his name was Richard he looked different somehow. Just like the night I found him in the garden.'

'What do you think, Mum?' asked Cliona.

'I don't know what to think any more. There's something happening that we can't explain. I just wish I had the answer.'

The Coopers had just finished their evening tea when Laura arrived back again.

'Brian got up for a little while,' Sheila told her. 'His appetite is fine, but he's so pale and lethargic that I told him to go back to bed.'

'That's not the only reason I came.' Laura's face was flushed and she asked, 'Did you read the paper today?'

'No, we didn't get one. Why?'

'Look,' Laura spread out the paper on the kitchen table in front of them. She had outlined a small item on page 4, in red ink, and Sheila read aloud:

> Dr Simon Harvey, the eminent psychologist from Georgia, USA, whose particular interest is the study of the paranormal, and who lectured in Dublin on Friday night, will be speaking at the Sligo Park Hotel, today, Monday, at 7 pm.

'Will you go?' asked Laura.

'What do you think, Ian? What's happening to Brian is certainly beyond our understanding of what is normal. Maybe this man could help us.'

'We could certainly do with some advice on what to do next, and I don't think the standard approach is the answer in Brian's case. But,' looking at his watch, 'we'd never make it in time now.'

'You could ring and ask if he'd see you after his talk,' suggested Laura 'Oh, please do. He may be the only one who can help.'

'Yes, something must be done. I'll ring him at once.'

'You're a good friend to Brian,' Sheila said as Ian left to phone, and then lapsed into silence.

'What did he say?' they both asked as soon as Ian opened the kitchen door again.

'Dr Harvey will see us in the hotel lounge after his talk. And he said to bring Brian along too.'

'Will you explain to him while I talk to the girls,' said Sheila. 'Tell them to come down.'

A few minutes later Cliona and Niamh rushed into the kitchen.

'Dad said you are going to Sligo to meet an American doctor,' said Cliona.

'Yes,' said Sheila, showing them the newspaper article.

'What does "paranormal" mean?' asked Niamh.

Sheila hesitated, trying to find the right words. 'I think it's any phenomenon that has not been explained by scientific principles.'

'Like ghosts?'

'Yes, like ghosts.'

'You better tell her what "phenomenon" means, too,' advised Cliona.

'I know that.' Niamh said smugly.

'Tell us then.'

'It is any remarkable place or thing.'

'That about sums it up,' said Sheila, smiling at Niamh's air of triumph. 'Just keep your fingers crossed that he can help. And now I really must hurry.'

Laura said she would babysit while they were away and Sheila rang and explained the situation to Paula, who was so sure it would solve everything that she felt almost light-hearted on the drive to Sligo. But Brian was quiet, and any attempts at conversation were met with monosyllabic replies, so they gave up. Sheila fervently hoped that he would be a bit more forthcoming with Dr Harvey.

She need not have worried. Simon Harvey, an inch or two taller than Ian's six-foot, with an unruly mop of brown curly hair, was the type of person who immediately made them feel at ease. Soon they were chatting away to him. They told him about Brian's visit to Ashbrook, of his arriving home in a confused state. Of being taken to Sligo hospital, how later he kept insisting his name was Richard Grier and not Richard Parry, and, finally, of their utter bewilderment when he found the missing land certificate.

Simon interrupted to ask a question now and again, but mainly he listened in thoughtful silence. When they finished he said, 'I know how worrying this must be for you, but from my point of view it's very interesting and I'm hopeful that I can help. I need to talk to Brian now though, so could you leave us alone for a little while?'

When they returned, Brian, to their relief, looked relaxed, the strained look gone.

'I think I can help,' said Simon. 'but I need some more information and it would mean another visit to Ashbrook. Luckily I had intended to take a few days' break so I'm not due back for a while.'

'Come and stay with us,' said Sheila, delighted.

'I'd need to read the doctor's full report on the case first – maybe, Ian, you could call the hospital and ask them to make the notes available. Then after I've read the medical report I'll talk again to Brian. Hopefully I'll be with you by mid-morning tomorrow.'

While Ian phoned Dr Hackett. Sheila hastily drew a route man to Rossmore and Fernhill. On the way home Brian was more talkative and Sheila and Ian smiled at each other in relief when he said, 'I like Simon. I think he's going to be able to make some sense out of what has been happening to me.'

Next morning, Brian was first to reach the front door when Niamh shouted from upstairs, 'There's a car coming.'

Ian was fretting about Ashbrook. 'We don't have permission to go into the house. I suppose it must belong to somebody. We'll be trespassing.'

'Trespassing?' echoed Sheila. 'We'll worry about that later. Surely nobody could object when we explain why we're there.'

Simon spent the morning talking to Brian, and later after lunch, when he was sitting with Sheila and Ian, he explained, 'I told Brian to rest for a couple of hours and I'd talk to him later, but now I'd like to see Ashbrook. Would just one of you come with me? I'd like to get the feeling of the house when it's quiet.'

'Ian, you go. I'll stay here in case Brian wants anything. Better ring Michael. He knows how to get in.'

'We may as well go across by the fields,' said Ian after phoning Michael, throwing a pair of wellies to Simon.

'Yes, we're less likely to be seen,' agreed Simon.

It had rained during the night and the fields were

muddy, but a high narrow grassy path, which ran along a mossy bank covered with ferns that had turned to yellow and grey, took them most of the way, and when they crossed their third stone ditch, Ashbrook came into view.

'Michael said he and David came back a few days after Brian had been here and found the door open. He must have left the house in a hurry,' said Ian, as he pulled away the board in front of the lock.

Inside, the two men paused to look around. 'It seems such a waste of a fine house. You would think Albert Parry would have sold the place if he didn't want to live here himself,' said Ian.

'Where is he now?'

'Probably still in South Africa.'

After taking a look around downstairs, they climbed the wide staircase, which creaked under their weight. 'Cliona said they found Brian through here,' said Ian, going to the door at the top of the stairs.

'Wait, I'd rather see the other rooms first. Usually I get a feeling in a place if anything unusual has happened in it,' explained Simon.

'I don't think much of Parry's taste in ornaments,' shuddered Ian as they passed the African mask.

Simon admired the fine view of the oak woods and the river from the two north-facing bedrooms, and from the third they both silently looked out at the tangled growth in the neglected garden below.

They retraced their steps along the corridor, and went into the L-shaped room. Then they looked into the study before returning.

'Yes, this one is different from the others. I could get faint vibes in the study, but here the feeling is much stronger.'

Simon, who was now standing in front of the fireplace looked around him and said slowly, 'Sometimes I get images as well.' Seeing Ian's startled expression he elaborated further. 'Psychometry. It's the ability to sense the history of an object, which in this case is a room. The word means "measurements made by the mind". I can see by the look on your face you're having difficulty believing me, but maybe in this instance you'll take my word for it. I've put it to the test quite a few times.'

'If you can find any clue in this house to bring Brian back to the way he used to be . . .' Ian's voice trailed away.

Simon smiled. 'You sit there on the window-sill while I concentrate for a little while.'

Ian sat quietly on the dusty window-sill. Looking down

at the letters carved into the wood he wondered about
Richard. What was he like, this boy whose identity Brian
had assumed? What had happened to him?

Suddenly Simon asked, 'Do you hear anything?'

'No, why? What is it?'

'Footsteps. Running downstairs.'

'I can't hear a thing,' whispered Ian, but Simon was not
listening. He was staring at the open door, his body rigid,
his face tense. Then he relaxed and turned away.

'You saw something?'

'Just for a moment. A tall thin woman. An unhappy face.
Calling in an anguished voice, "Richard!". Then she
disappeared.'

'Who do you think it was?'

'I think it was the ghost of Susannah Parry. And she was
calling for her son,' said Simon a little shakily. 'What really
happened to Richard, do you know?'

'I'm not sure. Jack said the story was that he ran away.'

'Usually,' explained Simon, 'a paranormal occurrence of
this type means that something violent could have taken
place. Maybe it took place here in this room.'

'You think Brian saw something here too, don't you?'
asked Ian.

'Yes. I do. And before I decide what should be done. I'd
really need to know more about Richard.'

Slowly they went down the stairs and left Ashbrook.

8
Mrs Clarke's Story

Brian was pushing Paul on the swing when Laura arrived.

'Dad and Simon are back from Ashbrook,' said Brian.

'Has Simon found out anything that will help?' Laura asked eagerly.

'I don't think so. He's in the study making notes now. 'I believe he told Mum that he would like to know what happened to Richard.'

'Richard seems to be the key to everything,' said Laura slowly. 'I've tried to find out about him but I'm up against a blank wall. Everyone just says that he ran away. End of story. It's all so vague. Susannah lived for a few years after Richard ran away. She must have talked to someone. Did Richard write to her? Surely he would have let her know where he was. If he did, wouldn't she have told him that Albert Parry had gone away and that he could come back.

'It's so frustrating. Somebody *must* know something.'

'That's what I can't understand,' said Brian. 'In a small place like this one would have thought that everyone would know what happened to the Parrys.'

'True. But, remember, when the fishing developed a lot of strangers came in, and somehow the old families faded into the background.'

'Old families?'

'The ones that have lived here for generations, and

didn't go away for years, like Dad and Ian's father. They know everything about everyone. Wait! . . . Why didn't I think of it before. Mrs Clarke: She's donkey's years old and her family has always lived in Rossmore. Right beside Ashbrook. Brian, let's go and see her.'

As they were walking along the road, Laura said, 'I'd better warn you about Mrs Clarke. She's a little bit peculiar, behaves oddly at times. Some of the children are afraid of her. And there's one other thing. She sometimes wears her hat when she's indoors, and it's got zips sewn all over it.'

'A hat made with zips. I don't believe it,' said Brian.

'She thinks it's style,' and they both laughed. But today when Mrs Clarke opened the door, after several minutes, she was not wearing her hat with the zips. Instead she had on a multi-coloured knitted one, pulled down over her ears and tied beneath the chin. If not exactly hostile, she was not exactly friendly.

'What do you want?' she asked brusquely.

'We were wondering,' began Laura, 'if you were living here at the time Susannah Parry's son, Richard, disappeared. Could you tell us what happened?'

'What do you want to know that for? It's all dead and gone now. Long ago. No point raking up the past.'

'It's for a project,' lied Laura. 'Brian and I are working on one. About the old houses in Rossmore.'

'Why do you want to do Ashbrook?' Mrs Clarke still sounded suspicious. 'It isn't as if it was Lough Deery Castle or Meenavalley. It's only an ordinary house.'

Laura had a sudden inspiration. 'Brian's father used to spend holidays with Peter – he was his grand-uncle. And he told him all about the Parrys, Susannah and Richard. We know most of the story. We only want to fill in a few details.'

'So you're related to Peter,' said Mrs Clarke, relaxing visibly and actually smiling at Brian. 'I remember your father well. Never met him but I used to see him around. Come on in and I'll tell you anything I can.'

'I think we've scored,' whispered Laura as she and Brian followed Mrs Clarke into the kitchen.

'Still wish I'd seen the hat with the zips,' grinned Brian.

In no time at all, the pair were sitting around the fire in Mrs Clarke's cosy kitchen, eating sultana scones.

'Poor Richard's favourites,' said Mrs Clarke. 'Many's the

time he used to sit there, just where you are now, and wolf them down. Poor lad. He had a hard time in Ashbrook.'

'It's Richard we really want to know about,' said Laura. 'Nobody seems to know what happened. Or if they do they aren't talking. My Dad says it's because some people felt they should have helped him more and didn't. What did happen? I know it's a long time ago but you must re- member something.'

'Of course I remember. It must be nearly forty years ago, but the night Richard disappeared is not one I'm likely to forget,' Mrs Clarke said with a sigh, and then she continued, 'It was this time of year, late October, when it happened. Susannah had gone into Rossmore that evening. Richard had a cold so she left him at home with Albert. When she came home the boy was gone. Seems he'd had a row with Albert and ran off.

'Susannah was distraught. She reported him missing right away, and the local sergeant organised search-parties and combed the area. My husband and Peter were with them. And Albert joined in the search.

'It was a very cold night. I did my best to comfort Susannah, but she refused to stay in Ashbrook or come here. Nothing would do her but to walk up and down the lane, and over and back the main road, and all the time she was calling for Richard.

'We could see the lights of the search-parties, spread out across the fields, down by the river, and over that large area of bogland that stretches behind my house. And everyone was calling his name over and over.

'The search was hampered that first night by the fog, and had to be called off until the next morning. They even brought fellows with tracker dogs in to help, but Richard was never found. The sergeant concluded he had been lost in the bog.

'Poor Susannah was like a creature demented. She lived on at Ashbrook, cutting herself off from almost everybody. She shunned visitors completely, even had her groceries delivered. She would only go out at night, and then she would walk up and down the lane with a torch, calling for Richard.

'Sometimes I would persuade her to come in and have some soup or a cup of tea, but towards the end she was not making much sense, and she was not taking care of herself properly. She carried on for five or six years, all alone. Then one morning the postman found her in the kitchen, in a chair beside the range, dead.'

There was silence for a little while when Mrs Clarke had finished speaking as Laura and Brian thought of what it must have been like on that cold October night almost forty years ago, feeling some of the deep anguish that Susannah Parry felt for the loss of her son.

It was Laura who spoke first. 'And that was the end of Susannah Parry, unless of course it's true that she haunts Ashbrook.'

'There was an old man who lived around here when she died, and he said her soul would never rest until she found her son.' Mrs Clarke got to her feet, and briskly poking the already blazing fire she murmered, 'Well, if there is a ghost – and I'm not saying there is – I'm not the only one to have seen it.'

'Did Susannah have any brothers or sisters?' Brian asked.

'There were two sisters, Charlotte and Lavinia. They both died the year before Susannah. The three girls and their mother were very popular in the area when they lived here. But the father, Ignatius Anderson, was not well liked.

He was a wool merchant. He made his money buying the wool cheap from the poor people and then selling it at a huge profit. And when he bought Ashbrook, a lot of people thought that he would have to pay for making money out of the poor. That no luck would come of it.

'Susannah was the youngest by many years, and the older two had been in America for some time when Ignatius Anderson lost Ashbrook to the bank. Susannah was devastated, she loved the place so much. But she could see no wrong in the father. They all moved to a cottage a few miles away, and she stayed with them and helped look after both of them when they got sick. By that time she was married to James Grier – that was her first husband. He died within a few years, and as her parents were also dead by that time, she went to live with Peter.'

'How did she come to marry Albert Parry?' asked Laura.

'Old Peter used to say it was to get back to Ashbrook – she really loved that house and wanted Richard to have it. It may have had something to do with it but I think she must have felt some affection for Albert. At least in the beginning. A big bear of a man, home from the mines in South Africa, lonely and all on his own. Susannah was very soft-hearted.

'He had a bad accident out there, by the way. Nearly lost his arm. He didn't, but it left him with a scar inside his right wrist. Maybe that added to his glamour.' Mrs Clarke's tone was dry.

'I've heard the marriage wasn't very happy,' said Brian.

'No more it was. Albert Parry turned out to be a cantankerous brute. Had to have his way in everything. Barney Flood – you know him, do you? – was about the closest he had to a friend and even he used to complain he was domineering.'

'What happened him – Parry?'

'He didn't stay in Rossmore too long after Richard disappeared. Went back to Africa it was said. People were surprised he let Susannah stay on in the house – that shows the kind of reputation he had. But I think he would have been lynched if he hadn't.'

'Did he come home when Susannah died?'

'Not that I know of.'

'What happened to all the things in the house?'

'It seems Albert sent instructions to his bank and his solicitors to pack up all the good stuff and store it. Three big removal vans arrived one day. There was a lot of excitement about it at the time and all the children from the locality were up at the house peeking in. Then Ashbrook was locked up, and every now and then a man would come and look it over. But it soon fell into decay. When I think of how much that house meant to Susannah! And just look at the state of the place now . . . Peter was right. She should never have married Parry. But when you've had one happy marriage – and she had with Grier – it's hard to think the second won't be like it.'

Brian suddenly put both hands to his head and Laura asked anxiously, 'Are you all right?'

'I've got a blinding headache again.'

'It *is* rather hot in here,' said Mrs Clarke sympathetically. 'You'll feel better when you get outside.'

'You've been such a help,' said Laura getting up. 'We don't know how to thank you.'

As she opened the door for them, Mrs Clarke paused for a moment. 'I often think they should have questioned Albert Parry more about that night. I think he had a lot more to do with Richard's disappearance than people realised.'

'Are you feeling any better?' asked Laura as they walked down the laneway in the crisp October air.

'A bit. The headache was building up for some time. Something happens when I hear the name Grier. It seems to have some peculiar effect on me.'

When they arrived back at the house, Simon, Ian and Sheila were in the kitchen, talking. Laura told them that they had been to see Mrs Clarke and that Brian had got one of his headaches again.

'Better lie down for a while,' counselled Simon, 'We can have our chat later.'

When Brian had gone upstairs, Laura said, 'Mrs Clarke thinks Albert Parry may have had something to do with Richard's disappearance. She didn't say murder, but I have a feeling that that's what she meant.'

'That would certainly explain a couple of things that have been bothering me,' said Simon with interest.

9

Ashbrook Revisited

When Simon went up to see Brian later, the curtains were closed. Brian was lying on the bed, staring at the ceiling.

'How do you feel now?' asked Simon.

'Fed up, and mixed up. I just don't know what to expect next. At first I was getting flashes and blurry pictures, moving so fast that I usually could not make them out. And then I'd get a terrible headache. This time it was just the headache. But when Mrs Clarke said "Grier" – and she said it twice – I was overcome with such a strong urge to shout, "My name is Richard Grier."

'I can't describe the feeling properly. It didn't last long, yet it seemed so real. But of course you all say I'm really Brian Cooper. I wish this was not happening. It's driving me mad.' Clenching his fists, he turned towards the wall.

'What about the time you found the papers in the trunk. How did you feel that time?'

'When Sheila mentioned the missing land certificate, I immediately pictured the trunk with the false bottom in the attic. I just knew the papers were there. After I found them I got a dreadful headache, and the feeling that I was Richard returned more strongly than ever . . . Did you know that Mrs Clarke thinks he might have been murdered?'

'Yes, Laura told me.'

'Do you think it's possible that Richard's spirit could have taken possession of me and that's why I can't remember who I am. Or do you think I could be going mad?' Brian asked fearfully.

'No, you're not going insane, Brian. But there is something strange happening, and we must find the answer. Now I want you to close your eyes, relax, and rest awhile. I must talk to your parents but I'll be back soon.'

Returning to the kitchen, he spoke to Sheila and Ian. 'I had intended to have a few more sessions with Brian before I made my final decision, but he's so tense I don't think it would benefit him to wait. It must be now.' He paused before saying, 'If we are ever to solve this mystery we will have to bring him back to Ashbrook, to that room upstairs, to find out what happened.'

'We both had a feeling that there wouldn't be a straightforward medical solution to Brian's problem, and I thought I was prepared to accept this. But now that the moment has come, I'm terrified,' confessed Sheila, adding. 'What if things go wrong and he gets worse?'

'I'm sorry, Sheila, but it's the only course of action I can think of that may be of help. I would like to go across this evening, because if this doesn't work I'll have to try to think of something else tomorrow. Would you both like to talk it over?'

'No, there's no need. We really don't have a choice,' said Ian. 'We must trust you.'

'The fact that Brian knew exactly where to find the missing papers indicates that we are not dealing with amnesia, and it's not a case of double personality. But keep your hopes up. I came across a similar case in the Philippines a few years ago and all ended well.'

'Will you and Ian be with him all the time?'

'We'll be with him of course, though I think it will be better if we wait in the smaller room. Don't worry, we'll keep a close watch on him.'

'Why don't you come with us?' said Ian to Sheila when Simon had gone upstairs to get Brian.

'No, two is quite enough. I'll stay here and make sure Samson doesn't follow Brian.'

When Simon came down with Brian, he said quietly to Ian, who was putting a large torch in his pocket, 'I would like to follow Brian's movements of last Friday as closely as possible, so if we get there a little while before it gets dark, it should be right.'

Cliona, Niamh and Paul stood with Sheila at the front door, and watched until the others were out of sight, and then, silently, turned and went indoors again.

'The house is in an awful mess,' Brian said as he followed Ian and Simon into Ashbrook.

'I know, but it's been empty for years and years,' said Ian, asking in concern, when Brian stumbled and rubbed his hand across his eyes, 'Are you all right?'

'My head aches. I'm going upstairs to my room,' replied Brian.

'Just go along with whatever he says,' advised Simon as they followed him upstairs and into the L-shaped room, where they found him kneeling in front of the fireplace.

'What on earth is he doing?' asked Ian.

'I think he's looking for something. Yes, see, he's lifting a piece of the floorboard.' Simon was unable to keep the excitement out of his voice.

'I don't believe it,' said Ian shakily. 'He's got a penknife in his hand.'

Brian seemed completely unaware of their presence.

Opening out the red-handled pocket-knife, he went to the window, where he knelt down and immediately became engrossed in carving deeply into the window sill.

'Better sit down, Ian. You've had quite a shock,' said Simon, leading him into the small study.

'I don't know what to think,' said Ian, his head in his hands. 'He's changed into another person. He doesn't seem to know we're here. He just keeps whittling away.'

'I think it's better not to disturb him for the present. You sit there, and I'll keep an eye on him.'

So, they waited, mainly in silence, Simon every now and again taking a look into the other room.

As darkness fell Ian switched on his torch and stood beside Simon. The wind had risen slightly, and together they listened to the lonely sound of the sheet of zinc banging against the outhouse wall.

Brian was still at the window, but as they watched, his

body suddenly stiffened, and he stopped carving and turned instead towards the bedroom door.

'Switch off the torch. Someone is coming,' whispered
Simon.

Ian immediately switched off the torch and they moved
further into the L-shaped room. Peeping around the corner
of the fireplace wall they watched as a bright beam of light
came around the door.

'There's nobody there. The light is moving of its own
accord,' Ian said in astonishment.

And as they watched in amazement, the light moved
across the wall and hovered in the corner above the bed.

'Can you feel the cold?' asked Simon.

And Ian did feel it, a deep penetrating chill that had not
been there earlier. And then they heard a sigh, a sound that
started on a low pitch, but increased in volume and went
on and on until it seemed to fill the whole room.

'Look,' said Simon, 'Brian's moving.' and as the two
men watched, the boy, staring vacantly in front of him,
moved towards the bed in the corner.

'Just leave him.' Simon held Ian's arm as he went to
follow.

'But I must get to him. He may be in danger.'

'No, this is not a malevolent force. I would feel it if it
was. Don't worry, I have seen something similar before.'

Simon was reassuring, but Ian was uneasy as he watched
his son get closer to the bed and the floating light.

Both men jumped when Brian suddenly let out a
piercing scream and shouted, 'David was right. This place
is haunted,' but before Simon or Ian could stop him, he
ran from the room, dropping the penknife in his haste, and
his footsteps could be heard pounding down the stairs.

Ian rushed across the room. But before he reached the

door an icy gust of wind swirled around him and slammed it shut. He grabbed the knob, but no matter how he turned or twisted it the door refused to open.

'I must go after him. I could get out through the window above the porch and climb down.' Ian ran back into the study, but the window was stuck.

'I didn't expect the door to close like that,' said Simon, 'but whatever happened here tonight, at least Brian seems to have come back to himself, because he mentioned David.' He added, 'I saw a light in the lane. Maybe he's gone that way. We'd better hurry, there's a rather thick fog coming down.'

'There was a fog the night Richard disappeared,' said Ian worriedly, as he picked up the low chair, and slammed it against the window, shattering the glass.

He carefully climbed through, on to the porch roof. Simon was about to follow, when Ian cried out in alarm and went crashing through the slates and rotten rafters. 'I'm caught between the joists. Can you pull me up?' he called.

Reaching out, Simon grasped his hand and managed to haul him to the safety of the damp window-sill.

'We'd better stick close to the wall,' said Ian, when he'd recovered. He made his way towards the side of the porch roof, swung himself over the edge, and dropped to the ground. Minutes later Simon joined him, and they lay for a moment to regain their breath, before jumping up and looking anxiously in the direction of the lane.

'I can't see any light,' said Ian, moving past the kitchen window.

'Look, there it is,' Simon pointed across the fields towards Fernhill.

10

A Light in the Mist

When Brian in his panic had run from the L-shaped room, he had been unaware of the presence of Ian and Simon. In his confused state of mind he thought that this was his first visit to Ashbrook, when he had taken up David and Kieran's dare.

And now the terror he remembered from that first time, when he had seen the light, felt the chill, and heard that swelling sound returned even more vividly than before.

He pounded down the stairs, wrenched open the glass-panelled door, and then he was pulling at the heavy front door, his fingernails breaking as he tugged, his breath coming in short gasps. He was reliving his dream, that awful nightmare that used to haunt him night after night. Only now it was real. He had such an overwhelming desire to get away from Ashbrook that he only paused briefly outside. The moon had disappeared behind a cloud, so he pulled his small torch from his pocket. Then he was off again, running down the twisted lane, the torchlight jumping desperately in front of him.

Suddenly he stopped. Without warning, a fog had come down, and standing still, on the rutted lane, he felt very afraid. As he looked about him in alarm, it seemed to him that the fog was growing denser and his weak torch was useless in penetrating the dense white mass that eddied about him. He wondered if he should turn back. But looking behind, he could see it was just as bad. He had to go on.

He knew he was in great danger. If he wandered from the laneway he could fall into the swollen stream or the river, or he could end up in the swampy bogland on the other side of the lane.

Cautiously he moved forward, gingerly feeling his way. He switched on his torch again even though the light was useless, but it made him feel less alone and afraid.

He crept slowly along, the fog swirling thickly and damply around him, and as he stopped to test his footing he fervently wished he was safely at home. In the distance a dog barked, and he shivered slightly. Were there dangerous strays roaming the hills?

He gave a loud cry of pain and dropped his torch as he felt something stabbing him in the chest and thighs. He was unable to move forward and, feeling around, he found he was being held back by three strands of barbed wire. He had strayed from the laneway, and was now completely lost. As he pulled himself free of the stabbing wire, undecided what to do next, he became aware of a new danger. Water was seeping over the top of his Doc boots. He must be in the swampy area, and as he fought to keep his feeling of panic under control, the fog lifted slightly and he could see a light moving to his left. His sense of relief was enormous. Thank goodness, someone was coming.

'Help! Can you hear me? I'm lost,' he shouted, glad that his voice sounded so steady.

'Over here. Can you see?' A woman's voice, faint yet clear, called across the wavering mist.

'It must be Mrs Clarke,' Brian thought in relief as he called back, 'Yes, just about.'

Gratefully he stumbled towards the light. He fell once, his feet rapidly sinking in the bog, and there was an awful gurgling, sucking sound when he wrenched himself free and headed towards the light again.

The woman said nothing. She shone her torch on his face and indicated the way ahead.

When he eventually reached the safety of the laneway, he felt he should identify himself. 'We live at Fernhill. I was on my way home when the fog came down suddenly and I got hopelessly lost,' he explained, deciding not to tell of his visit to Ashbrook. Anyway, it was not something he wanted to think about himself yet. Later, when he was safely home, he'd think about it.

They walked along in silence. Brian was now able to see the thick trunks of the sycamore and chestnut-trees through the fog. Further along, in his right, he could see the grey shape of Ashbrook rising out of the fog. And when the wind rose, he could hear the clang of the corrugated sheet of zinc against the outhouse wall. He looked quickly away again, and shivering slightly, he wondered how many secrets that house held.

Would Michael, David and Kieran ever believe him? he wondered as he clambered over another stone ditch in the wake of his rescuer. The fog was not quite as dense, but visibility was still limited, and he was glad of the bright light the woman held, as they travelled the slippery, grassy path. It seemed to him to be an old-fashioned lamp rather than a torch. Probably Mrs Clarke felt it gave better light.

On their right, stunted trees grew on a mossy bank, their bare branches, like contorted limbs, etched momentarily by the light as they passed. And underneath some rowan-trees, on a high heather-covered bank, nestled some low bilberry bushes, safe from the wind, their delicate branches

bare until spring, when they would be covered in tiny oval leaves, and later small, pink, globe-shaped blossoms that would give way to masses of blue-black berries. They passed another clump of bare trees, where, in summer, the ground beneath them would be carpeted with bluebells. On their left was an old lime kiln, long overgrown with brambles, where some small ash-trees had found a precarious roothold.

Down a wet slope they went, past a birchwood, and then the woman halted. 'There.' She had stopped at a narrow gap in the hawthorn hedge. Looking in the direction she was pointing, Brian could at last see Fernhill. He was almost there. The fog had lifted, but it was very dark and he was glad to see that the light was on outside the house. A sob of relief caught in his throat as he turned to thank the woman. But there was no one there. She had vanished.

And then he heard it again, the plaintive sigh that started in a whisper, rising until it filled the air about him. And suddenly he was cold, very cold. For a moment he saw the light that had guided him home. It moved jerkily, high up in the trees, and then it was gone. The sighing stopped and the air about him grew warmer again. He was standing alone at the gap in the hawthorn hedge.

Wearily he rubbed his hand across his eyes. Then he jumped nervously when he heard a movement in the trees nearby. Peering into the darkness he could see nothing. Probably a badger or a fox he thought, as he began to walk through the gap. But suddenly, there was a louder noise, very close by, and he was grabbed roughly from behind. He screamed and struggled desperately to free himself. He managed to kick his assailant once on the leg, but as two powerful hands clasped tighter around his neck he knew he was no match for his attacker. He felt himself weakening.

And as his knees began to buckle, and his senses swim, he wondered in astonishment, who could possibly want to kill him.

Suddenly, out of nowhere, a brown ball hurled itself through the hedge with an angry bark, and Brian croaked gratefully, 'Samson, good boy.'

The unknown assailant yelled in pain as Samson sank his teeth into his arm, and his hold on Brian slackened. And through a haze he saw another light, and this time he could hear his father's voice calling him.

His attacker heard too, and suddenly releasing Brian he crashed through the trees. His hurrying footsteps could be heard on the lane close by, before they were lost in the clamour of Ian's anxious questions as he rushed to Brian's side, while Sampson hovered protectively above him.

'Are you all right, Brian? What happened?' Ian's voice was filled with concern.

'Take it easy, Ian. Give him a chance to get his breath back,' said Simon.

'Dad, someone just tried to kill me. He had his hands around my neck. It hurts,' Brian whispered through an aching throat.

'There was quite a scuffle,' said Simon, shining his torch on the ground. He pushed his way through the gap in the hedge, and went up the lane shining his torch to either side but returned in a couple of minutes saying, 'Whoever it was is long since gone. We'd better get Brian home to bed.'

'Cliona, I saw Susannah Parry – twice. I really did,' Brian said with a hoarse laugh, when he was lying back in bed recovering from his ordeal. 'The second time I saw her I thought it was Mrs Clarke on the lane. I was sure I'd left her ghost behind in Ashbrook. Do you think Michael and David and Kieran will believe me?'

'They'll believe you.' Cliona and Niamh spoke together..

'Mum, I must have left my school-bag at Ashbrook this evening, but I'll get it tomorrow.'

'Brian, it's days since you were in Ashbrook for the first time. And you had your school-bag home with you. You have been suffering from loss of memory,' Sheila said gently.

'And you've been calling yourself Richard Grier, and you said you did not know any of us,' put in Niamh, tremulously.

'That's weird, Niamh. I don't remember that at all.'

'Barney thought it was weird too,' said Cliona. 'I met him today and he asked how you were. I told him you were fine – except for calling yourself Richard Grier. And now that you know you're not, he'll think you're really nuts.'

'What about letting Brian rest now. Dr Boyle is coming out to see him later, and he told me on the phone to keep him quiet.' Ian was at the bedroom door.

'I'd like to ask Brian a few questions if I may,' Simon, who had been standing behind Ian, said.

'Oh, fine.' Then seeing Brian's blank expression, Ian asked, 'Do you remember meeting Dr Harvey in Sligo?'

Brian shook his head, and Ian explained about Laura seeing the article in the paper, and of their visit to Sligo.

'I won't be long,' Simon promised and he sat on the side of the bed and explained to Brian his involvement in the case.

'It's all so very strange. I don't remember any of it. But I would love to know more about Richard.' He added nervously, 'It looks as if it's not over yet though. Who on earth would want to kill *me*?'

'That's another mystery. Maybe you know something, or have seen something that could be a threat to someone. But try not to worry about it. Sergeant Coleman has your statement and he's promised they'll keep a close watch on this area. So, rest now, because Dr Boyle will be in soon.'

Later, when Dr Boyle had examined Brian, and had been brought up to date with the latest developments, he said to Simon as he was leaving, 'This has turned out to be the strangest case of my whole career. Will you give Dr Hackett and me full written reports. This is something we will want to go over in great detail.'

Having promised the reports, Simon joined the others in the sitting-room, and Ian poured him a large whiskey.

'We're still talking about Brian. It's so wonderful that he's back to normal again. But who could possibly want to kill him?' said Sheila shakily, and without waiting for an answer she continued, 'Samson seems to have sensed something. He kept jumping at the door barking, even though Cliona had taken him for a walk earlier. I was afraid to let him out in case he'd go across to Ashbrook and create difficulties for you. In the end it was Paul who opened the door. Anyway Brian's safe but I wonder when we will be able to say that this whole episode is definitely over ... We have so much to thank you for, Simon. You have been such a help. Brian had confidence in you, and you kept us calm through the whole thing. So many strange things have happened . . . Ian told me about Brian getting the penknife and carving into the window-sill.'

'Yes, What he actually did was put an "X" through the initials R.I.P., leaving only the letters R.G. There seems to have been a lot of anger there directed at Albert Parry. Maybe Mrs Clarke is right, and he did kill Richard. I don't have any clear-cut explanations. Most people are either sceptical or uncomfortable at the mention of the paranormal, but parapsychology has been a great interest of mine for years, and one day I expect it will become an accepted branch of science.

'The word paranormal really means impossible. Or impossible in terms of our usual theory of reality. But parapsychologists have demonstrated, time and again, the occurrence of these so-called impossible events.

'I think we must explore and change our definition of reality, because that is what decides what is possible and what is impossible. Maybe there are worlds beyond the one we live in. Worlds where time and space have not the same meanings. I'd say the answers are there, but we're not asking the right questions ... Sorry, I always get carried away when I'm on this subject,' he apologised. 'Now I'm off to bed. I'm rather tired.'

Sheila and Ian sat talking for a little longer and Sheila said, 'We have so much to be grateful for. Brian is okay, and we don't have to worry about the land certificate any more. If only we could clear up this business of why anyone is trying to harm Brian. Do you think it's in any way connected with Richard?'

'I can't see how. And I think you have done enough worrying. Let's sleep on it and maybe we'll come up with a likely answer in the morning,' said Ian, giving her a hug.

11
Richard's Diary

Next morning the children were up early, and when Ian and Sheila were getting dressed they could hear the sound of laughter coming from Brian's bedroom. The October sunshine was streaming in through the windows and it seemed impossible to think that there could still be a sinister shadow hanging over the family.

'Things are getting back to normal,' Ian smiled at Sheila and they went to see how Brian was feeling. He was propped up in bed, and Cliona, Niamh and Paul, still in their pyjamas, were bringing him up to date on all that had happened..

Later in the morning, Laura and Michael arrived and were allowed upstairs to see Brian, providing they didn't stay too long.

Jack stayed downstairs for a chat.

Michael wanted to hear all the details of the attack and see for himself the bruises on Brian's neck. 'Someone certainly grabbed you by the neck,' he said. 'But who would want to kill *you*.'

'I don't know. I've been going over and over it in my mind, but I can't think of anyone,' replied Brian.

'The important thing is that you're safe. And you're back to yourself again. We're thrilled about that,' said Laura with a smile.

'Thanks to you, Laura. If you hadn't seen that article in the paper about Simon, I'd probably still think I was Richard.'

'That reminds me. Look what I just took from Paul. He said he found it on the floor, the night of your first visit to Ashbrook. He kept it because he liked the colour of the cover. It looks like Richard's diary.' Laura handed him the dark blue diary, with the faded gold lettering.

'I'd forgotten all about it. I found it in an old brown armchair, in the L-shaped room. I put it in my jacket pocket, meaning to have a look at it later. It must have fallen out of my pocket,' said Brian excitedly, flicking through the mildewed pages. 'Now maybe we'll find out about Richard.'

'Read the first entry,' said Laura.

'It's a five-year diary. Starts on April 7 – it doesn't give the year, just the month.'

April 7:– 'I'm seven today. Peter gave me this diary for my birthday. I like it, and I'll keep it forever. Peter is nice. Mammy and me live with him and his mother, because Daddy is dead. Mammy gave me a football.

'Just keep reading,' said Laura, and Brian continued:

May 28:– Mammy brought me to meet a friend of hers today. His name is Albert Parry. He lives in Ashbrook, her old home. He didn't talk much to me.

June 23:– Tonight was bonfire night. We had ours built on the high field, so it could be seen for miles around.

We went to visit Albert Parry again this afternoon. I don't like him. but he and Mammy like each other.

August 4:– We went to Carnmore beach today. It was very hot. Peter is teaching me how to swim.

October 30:– Tea again with Albert Parry. I wanted to go into Rossmore with Peter, but Mammy said I must go to Ashbrook with her.

December 25:– Mammy told me that she is going to marry Albert Parry in the spring. Peter is very upset. I don't want to move from here, although Peter says I must visit them as often as I like.

Santa came last night. I didn't hear a thing. I got a jig-saw, Meccano, chocolate, lead soldiers, marbles and two books, *Robinson Crusoe* and *Treasure Island*. Mammy said she'd help me read them.

January 16:– We went to Ashbrook again today. This was my first time upstairs. Mammy and Albert wanted me to see my room. It's big and L-shaped, with a fireplace, and there's a small study off it. Mammy and her sisters used it when they were children. It's a nice room. The whole house is nice. But I don't like Albert. I think he's sly.

March 31:– My mother has married Albert and I'm called Richard Parry now instead of Richard Grier. I'm going to miss Peter and Fernhill.

April 10:– Albert took us into Rossmore on my birthday. He gave me money to buy comics.

July 6:– I have been sick with bronchitis for a few weeks and missed school. My mother has been worried. I don't think Albert cares though. He is only nice to me when my mother is around.

September 8:– We went to see Peter today, and I played in the attic. Albert was angry when we got back. He said we're going to Fernhill too often, that Ashbrook is our home now.

November 11:– I think Albert has been reading my diary, so I've found a hiding-place for it. Sometimes I think he hates me. He just sits and stares.

December 28:– Albert took us to Letterkenny last week to do our Christmas shopping. Santa came and brought me some more Meccano and soldiers and books. It wasn't much fun this year, but Mammy and I went to see Peter on Boxing Day. He was glad to see us, and he gave me a pocket knife with a red handle. I'll hide it with my diary.

February 14:– I've been sick twice since I went back to school, and my mother says she will teach me at home from now on. I'd rather go to school, but Albert says that as long as I'm under his roof I'm to do as I'm told. He's been searching my room for my diary, but he'll never guess the hiding-place. I do love this room though, and my mother puts on a fire for me every day.

'I'm going to skip a couple of years. It's all much the same and his writing is much easier to read towards the end,' said Brian as he flicked through the last pages of the diary before continuing:

November 30:– It has been snowing this past few days. I went sleighing on the high field yesterday, and when I was there a flock of wild geese flew overhead. They make such a lonely sound. I would have liked to call and see Peter, but I was afraid Albert might find out.

December 26:– Christmas was very quiet this year, but my mother and I decorated a small tree in the sitting-room. We kept a good fire on all day, and it was nice. I got a large train set and I've laid it out on my bed-room floor.

My mother and I went to see Peter yesterday. I heard him tell her that I should be mixing with children of my own age, but nobody calls to this house anymore.

January 18:– After Mass, I spent most of the day reading. I went down to the sitting-room a couple of times, but Albert kept giving me such horrible stares, that I went back to my room again. I think he hates me.

March 22:– I've been sick again, so I have not written anything in weeks. My mother sits with me a lot and reads to me. Sometimes, when I wake after dozing, Albert is standing at the bedroom door, staring at me. I'm afraid he will find the hiding-place for my diary.

April 10:– I got a new fishing-rod for my birthday. I went fishing yesterday and caught two trout. It's not the same without Peter though.

June 20:– I have been working in the garden this past few weeks. I have been trying to rebuild part of the garden wall that is crumbling. My mother says we may have to get a stone mason to do it next year. Albert watches me from the sitting-room window. I think he may be mad.

August 13:– I broke a jug this morning. Albert flew into a rage and hit me. I can always tell now, when he's working himself into a temper. When he's very angry he rubs the inside of his right wrist with his left index finger.

September 23:– Albert and I had an argument about my initials today. He wants me to use my second name which is Ignatius, after my grandfather. I never used it when I was called Grier. Albert wants me to use it now, so my initials read R.I.P., which I've carved on the bedroom window sill. But underneath I put R.G. because no matter what Albert may say, my name is Richard Grier.

We went into Rossmore to do our shopping today. Albert just sat in the car frowning. Nobody bothers to stop and talk to him now. I helped my mother to carry the shopping. She has got very thin.

October 30:– When we came home from Mass today, I knew Albert had been searching my room, because things were moved. He must be still looking for my diary. He really is mad.

I couldn't eat much dinner today, because each time I looked up I found Albert staring at me. I spent most of the day in my room.

October 31:– When I woke this morning, I found Albert standing in the doorway looking at me. Later, I asked my mother if we could go back to Peter's, where we were happy. She said she'd think about it.

But I'm afraid Albert may have overheard us. I'm sure I heard a noise outside the kitchen door. I wish my mother was back, but she's late. She had to go into Rossmore. She wouldn't let me go with her because my cough has started again.

There's someone coming up the stairs. Heavy footsteps, and they have stopped outside my door. I must hide my . . .

'That's all there is,' said Brian, with a catch in his voice.

'Richard musn't have had time to put his diary in the usual place with his penknife, so he stuck it down the back of the armchair . . . Simon told me where the penknife had been kept.'

'It looks as if Mrs Clarke could be right,' said Laura, and then realising that Brian had no memory of their visit, she repeated the conversation to him.

'Poor Richard. I wish we really knew what happened. If he is dead, his body should be laid to rest, and then Susannah too would be at peace. I wonder if she thought I was Richard when she led me out of the fog to safety.' Brian said sadly.

'Come on, Brian. It's over and you're safe. Forget about it now,' pleaded Michael.

'Yes, it's better not to brood about these things,' agreed Laura.

'I suppose you're right. It's in the past.' Brian closed the diary and rubbed his fingers gently over the faded gold letters. 'It's the present I should be thinking of, and I promised Paul I'd go to the Hallowe'en party in the parish hall with him, and that's what I'm going to do.'

'Are you sure you're up to it?' asked Sheila doubtfully when Brian told her of his plans.

'Yes, I'm fine. My throat's still sore, but I'm not an invalid you know.'

'Sounds like the old Brian,' she said with a smile.

'I think he should go. It will take his mind off his ordeal,' agreed Ian.

'Yes, the best thing for Brian now is to get involved in normal activities again,' said Simon.

'Will you come to the Hallowe'en party, Simon?' asked Brian.

'Yes, do come. I've promised to sell raffle-tickets, so you can help. *We* don't have to dress up,' said Ian with a smile.

'There's a competition to find the best pumpkin and I'm one of the judges. I know the others would be delighted with an American opinion, so do come,' invited Sheila.

'Count me in!'

'I must go into town to collect our pumpkin now, and I'd like some volunteers to help get our Jack o'lanterns ready when I get back,' said Sheila, hurrying off.

'Tell her to wait for me, I must go into Rossmore to get a mask.' Brian jumped out of bed and began dressing.

Simon and Ian smiled at each other. Obviously he was making a rapid recovery.

Brian chose a Dracula mask, which covered his face and hair and gave him a frightening appearance, so he was very happy with it. When he was paying at the cash desk in the shop he glanced out of the window and saw Barney looking in. He smiled and waved, but Barney did not return the wave. Instead, he stood there, frowning, and stared at Brian for an uncomfortably long time before turning suddenly and walking away.

Shaken, Brian left the shop. 'I don't think Barney likes me,' he said to Sheila as they walked to the car.

'Barney? I'm beginning to think he's a head case. He acts so strangely at times.'

Back at Fernhill Simon and Brian scooped the fruit from the pumpkin, and while Cliona was cutting the large triangular nose and eyes and long jagged mouth, Niamh went in search of a candle. Sheila had bought two barmbracks, and they had an early tea. It was a noisy meal, the children talking excitedly about the forthcoming party. Later, when they got dressed in their costumes, Simon took photographs.

Brian had found a long black evening cape in the attic. It had a soft high collar and he wore it over his black jeans and polo neck.

Cliona and Niamh were both dressed as witches, with hideous faces and hooked noses. Niamh's mask had masses of red curls while Cliona's had long grey floating locks.

Paul was all in black, his face hidden behind a gaunt mask with horns on top. He was holding a long-handled toasting fork and anxiously asked, 'Do I look like a real devil?'

'The genuine article,' teased Brian, pricking him with his fork.

The hall, decorated with colourful streamers and balloons, was already half full when they arrived, and Ian placed their pumpkin alongside the others on the long tables set against one wall. Other tables were laden with food and drink.

Soon the large room was filled with witches, wizards, black cats, mummies, monsters, goblins, devils, knaves, and even a couple of druids. There was a hum of excitement as they all milled around, trying to identify friends. Later, there would be a prize for best mask and another for best costume. Then the masks would be left off and everyone would eat.

Nobody had noticed the tall figure that had detached himself from the shadows outside, and joined the last group entering the hall.

12
Unmasked!

Laura and Michael knew what costumes the Coopers were wearing, so they did not have too much trouble finding them. Laura was also dressed as a witch. Her mask had thick black curls, and like Cliona and Niamh she wore a long brightly coloured skirt and blouse.

'It will be fun when everyone takes their masks off. I'm sure David and Kieran are here, and I'd love to find out who that very tall fellow with the werewolf's mask is. Every time I turn around I see him,' said Brian to Laura.

They had a look at the pumpkins lined up on the tables, each with a coloured candle inside. 'The candles will be lit shortly, and the lights will be switched off while the judging takes place,' explained Laura, shouting to make herself heard above the din.

Brian did not want to miss the judging of the lanterns, but he needed to go to the loo first, so he made his way to the double doors beside the stage, and along the corridor to the cloakroom. He was on his way back when the lights went out. He stood still, mask in hand, annoyed that he might miss the judging, and waited impatiently for them to come on again.

He was standing beside a store-room door, which was ajar, and it was not until he heard the creak as it opened further that he realised he was not alone.

He felt his mouth going dry, but before the first rush of fear had coursed through his body, he was roughly grabbed from behind. He tore at the mask his assailant was wearing but he could not escape. He was hauled into the store-room and he heard a key turn in the lock. The waxing moon dimly illuminated part of the room, and when Brian regained his balance, he found he had a werewolf's mask in his hands.

He looked over at his attacker.

It was Barney!

'Barney! Why? Why are you attacking me?' asked Brian desperately.

Just then the lights came on again.

Barney's sleeve had fallen back, and on the inside of his wrist there was a large scar, which the man was absent-mindedly rubbing with the index finger of his left hand.

A scar, just inside the right wrist? Brian fought to remember. Who had talked about a scar? Of course! It was Laura, the day she had told him about their visit to Mrs. Clarke, which he had forgotten. She had mentioned Albert Parry and his accident at the mines. He could hear her saying in a grim voice, 'So, if you ever meet a tall chap with a scar on the inside of his right wrist, watch out! Or you too will end up in a bog-hole.'

As he watched in horrified fascination, unable to move, the man advanced towards him.

'You're not Barney,' Brian blurted out. 'You're Albert Parry!'

'You knew all along, didn't you,' said Albert.

'No, I didn't know. Honestly. Until now I thought you were Barney Flood.'

'Cliona told me that after your first visit to Ashbrook you thought your name was Richard Grier. You *are*

Richard Grier. You've come back to haunt me. Did Susannah send you?'

'No, no, I'm Brian. I was suffering from loss of memory,' he said, backing away.

But there was a gleam of madness in Albert's eyes as he kept advancing towards the retreating boy, and he spoke in a low menacing tone. 'I thought I'd killed you, Richard. You were trying to get Susannah to leave me. And now you have come back to torment me, so I must kill you again.'

Brian's face and hair was drenched in perspiration as he tried to evade the strong hands that reached out for his neck, but Albert lunged and caught him. As Brian struggled, he wondered desperately if he were going to die and whether anyone would ever know the truth about Albert Parry.

Meanwhile, back in the hall, Laura was wondering what had happened to Brian.

'He said he wanted to see the lanterns when they were lit. And he's missed that. And now everyone has their masks off, and they're going to eat,' she said to Cliona.

'I don't see the very tall fellow with the werewolf's mask around either. Brian was anxious to know who he was,' said Michael, looking about him.

Laura turned pale and said, 'We'd better find Ian and Simon. Something is badly wrong.'

They pushed their way through the crowd, keeping an eye out for Brian as they went, but by the time they had reached the two men,. they still had not found him.

Urgently Laura explained her worries.

'I saw Brian going out through the door beside the stage a little while ago.'

'Did he not come back?' asked Simon.

'No, and we can't find him,' said Laura.

'I'm going to look for him.' Ian barely waited for Laura to finish. He hurried towards the doors, leaving the others to follow.

He was already checking the cloakroom when the rest caught up with him.

'He's not here,' he said grimly, and started down the corridor again.

As they were passing the store-room door, Simon suddenly stopped and asked, 'Did you hear anything?'

They stood listening for a moment. 'I think I heard a noise but the door's locked,' said Ian, trying the handle. 'Brian, are you all right?' he called anxiously, but all they could hear was a muffled sound.

'I'm going to have to break it open,' he said, as he kicked hard just below the lock. Simon helped, and the door burst open, sending them headlong into the room.

Barney turned in surprise, his face contorted with fury, and before Brian lost consciousness, he said weakly, 'Don't let him get away, Dad. He's really Albert Parry, and he murdered Richard.'

Ian dived for Albert, and Michael went to help. Simon went to Brian's assistance, and Laura, Cliona and Niamh ran to get Dr Boyle and Sergeant Coleman.

Brian had recovered consciousness by the time Sheila arrived with Dr Boyle, who ordered him to bed. 'You're going to be sore for a while, but you're a lucky boy.'

Albert Parry was led away, his head bowed. He looked at nobody.

Sheila was still in a state of shock. 'I can't believe it. All this time, Barney was really Albert Parry.'

'And it was I who told him about Brian thinking he was Richard Grier,' said Cliona. 'And it was that night that the first attempt was made to kill him.'

Ian brought the car around, and they left quietly by a side door. Back at Fernhill, Brian was put to bed straightway and, totally exhausted, he was asleep in minutes. Ian had filled in some of the details of the case for Sergeant Coleman, who said he would call back in the morning for Brian's statement.

Next morning Brian's throat was very sore. He could only speak in a hoarse whisper but he was able to make a statement when the Sergeant arrived..

Later, downstairs in the kitchen, Sheila asked, 'Why did Albert want to murder poor Richard anyway?'

Between Brian and Albert Parry Sergeant Coleman had pieced together most of the puzzle:

'It seems Albert heard Richard begging his mother to leave Ashbrook and go back to Fernhill. And that evening, when Susannah was late getting back from Rossmore, Albert lost control completely. Convinced that she was not coming home, he took a heavy walking-stick from the umbrella-stand in the hall, and went upstairs and confronted Richard.

'He hit Richard once, on the head, in the bedroom. And when the boy ran downstairs and out through the door Albert followed. It was almost dark and there was a fog coming down, and Richard wandered off the lane. Albert said he could hear him calling for help, that he was sinking in the bog. Following the voice, Albert found the poor boy, hit him again, and then pushed him deeper into the bog.

'Albert now says that after that the night is a blank. He has, for instance, no memory of taking the large torch from the porch with him, but he must have had it to find his way back. He doesn't remember getting home, but he was sitting in the kitchen, wondering what to do next, when Susannah returned.

'She explained that, first a flat tyre and then the fog, had delayed her. She had got a new bottle of cough mixture for Richard.

'At that stage Albert decided he had to cover up. He told Susannah that he'd had a row with Richard, who'd run away. That he had searched, but could not find him.'

'So, now you have a confession but no body,' said Ian.

'Yes, that's right. Albert says he can't remember exactly where it happened. And there's a large area of bogland out there. But Dr Harvey here says he can help us.'

'Have you done much missing person work?' Ian asked.

'I've helped with quite a few cases in America, but this will be my first one in this country.'

'Won't you need something belonging to Richard?'

'I have something. The red-handled pocket-knife. I took it with me that night we were at Ashbrook,' explained Simon.

Later that day Laura and Michael came over and the children gathered in Brian's bedroom to discuss the Hallowe'en party and its terrifying climax.

'So Barney is really Albert Parry. It's so hard to believe that he's been living back here all these years and nobody ever guessed it,' said Michael.

'And Brian Cooper has only been here a couple of months – and he has unravelled the mystery,' put in Laura.

'Not quite unaided,' said Brian, whose voice was still hoarse. 'Only for Laura, we would never have gone to see Mrs Clarke and never found out about Richard.'

Samson who was lying at the door barked and wagged his tail. 'I think he's reminding me how he saved me the first time I was attacked,' grinned Brian.

'Come on, I think that's enough talking for now. Mum says Brian is to rest his voice,' said Cliona protectively.

'Hang on a minute!' Brian sat up in bed, his face flushed. 'There's something else we must do. I want to see where Richard's body has been all these years. That is, if they find it.'

'I think Simon will be able to locate it. He's helped the police with lots of cases in America.'

'Well he certainly helped me.' Brian sank back into the pillows and closed his eyes, as the others left, gently closing the door behind them.

When they told Sheila that they wanted to watch the

search for Richard's body, she was doubtful at first. 'I don't think Brian is really feeling up to it, no matter what he says,' she demurred 'And I was hoping we could keep the search a secret. We don't want sensation seekers.'

'I don't think that would be true in this case. A great many people have been involved from the beginning, and they have a genuine interest. Some have volunteered to help if they are needed,' said Ian.

'You're right.' agreed Sheila. 'Anyway we can't stop them.'

Word of the impending search had spread like wildfire around the immediate area, into Rossmore and beyond,

and people had come out to watch, huddling in quiet groups in the chilly November air.

The bottom part of the lane to Ashbrook was thronged with onlookers when Ian arrived with the children. As he walked along the lane his mind was on Albert Parry. The man who had shunned the society of his neighbours had, by his actions, become the centre of attention.

A section of the bog had been cordoned off with blue and white tape, and a garda with a log-book was writing down the names of those permitted to enter. Simon, standing just inside the sealed-off area, was being interviewed by newspaper reporters. Then he moved off to talk to Sergeant Coleman, who had a map of the area spread out on the roof of the white garda car. He had already studied it in the garda station, but he pored over it again, concentrating deeply, all the time holding the red-handled pocket-knife. After a short time he pointed to a particular area on the map and Sergeant Coleman gave instructions to four gardai who were wearing waders.

They each took a spade, and crossed a stone ditch into the bogland. They had not gone very far when they came to a clump of silver birch. They stopped beside the largest tree, and there they started to dig.

Time passed. People were moving about now, stamping their feet to restore the circulation, and quietly talking to each other.

'Look, the sergeant is on his walkie-talkie.' It was Brain who spoke, then he lapsed into silence again as they waited tensely.

The crowd was getting restless, and some had gone home by the time a large car arrived. Two men got out and came up the lane to the sergeant, who had wellies waiting for them. 'That's the state pathologist on the left. I read in the paper that he was to be in Letterkenny today, so he didn't have too far to come,' Ian said quietly to the children, and they watched as the men crossed the ditch, and joined the gardai beside the silver birch.

The gardai emerged from the trees, and a sigh ran through the onlookers when they saw them carry something wrapped in thick green plastic to the waiting ambulance. As the crowd began to move away, singly and in pairs, some of the older ones blessed themselves and said it was a good thing his body was recovered today – All Souls' Day. But there was a sad shaking of heads, because now everyone knew for sure what had happened to Richard.

'Come on, we've seen enough. Let's go home,' said Ian to the subdued children at his side.

'Simon knew exactly where they should look,' thought Brian as they walked up the lane to take the short way home.

They stopped for a moment to look at Ashbrook. The house that had at last yielded up its secret stood silent and brooding, its windows blank and vacant. Susannah Parry would never run down its tangled avenue again. They did not linger, but moved on quickly across the fields to the warmth of Fernhill, where Sheila was waiting with Paul. Michael and Laura had gone home, and Cliona and Niamh had run ahead to tell her that the body had been found.

'Poor Richard. It's so sad, but I do feel better knowing that now he can get a proper burial,' said Sheila, handing round mugs of hot soup.

They were all sitting glumly in the kitchen later when Simon and Sergeant Coleman came in. 'Well, it looks as if we now have the answer to a forty-year-old mystery,' said

Simon, settling himself by the fire with a cup of coffee.

'But why did Albert Parry come back at all, and why did he pretend to be Barney Flood? And what happened to the real Barney Flood?' Brian asked in a rush.

'Brian, that's three questions together,' laughed Ian, 'but maybe the sergeant has some of the answers for you.'

'Yes, as it happens I do have most of the answers now. All Albert wants to do at the moment is talk. He says he's glad it's all over and that he's been caught.

'When Albert left here, shortly after Richard's disappearance, he went back to Africa. Some time after that Barney followed, and they worked together for a while. Albert had probably intended to stay away for good – he knew nobody wanted him around here and that people were saying that Susannah had died from a broken heart and that he was the cause. Then he got a letter from a mining company saying that a geological survey of the area had shown silver deposits on his land, and they wanted to meet and discuss terms. So he decided to come back, just for a short time.

'Barney Flood decided to come home with him – for good. He had a little nest-egg piled up and said he would be comfortable for life. On the boat from Holyhead to Dun Laoghaire the two men had a few drinks together. The sea became rough, and Albert says that Barney decided to go on deck for some fresh air as he felt queasy. He had been gone for some time when Albert decided to go and look for him. He found him leaning over the rail. The ship was tossing a lot as the sea had become rougher, and before Albert could reach him, Barney had bent over a fraction too far and he fell overboard.'

There was silence for a moment, and then Cliona asked in a hushed voice, 'Do you think Albert pushed him?'

'No, I think it could have happened that way. Albert seems to want to tell the truth at this stage. He says his first thought was to get the captain to stop the ship and turn back and search, but he knew Barney did not stand a chance in such seas.

'And then, he says, it came to him all of a sudden. He would become Barney Flood. Barney had been well-known in Rossmore. He was accepted. It was known he had gone to South Africa and no one would be surprised at his return – he'd done it a few times before. Best of all, he had no relatives.

'Albert collected Barney's luggage off the ship, as well as his own. He decided to stay in Dublin for a while to perfect his disguise. It wasn't difficult. People had often remarked how alike he and Barney looked. They were almost the same height, and they both had wiry grey hair. All he had to do was grow a beard like Barney. Not that he was too worried about the appearance side of it. Barney had been away for several years so it was unlikely people would remember exactly how he looked. And he also practised Barney's signature until he had it right.

'While he was in Dublin waiting for his beard to grow, he put the second part of his plan into action. He went to see his solicitors and made arrangements with them to hold his mail for him, using the excuse that he'd be moving around a lot, and would collect it each time he returned to Dublin.

'So Albert's deception began. He would be known as Barney Flood in Rossmore, and he could quietly keep an eye on Ashbrook and any mining that might take place. And in Dublin, he'd be known as Albert Parry and take care of any business dealings with the mining company there, through his solicitors. He says it was all so easy. He admits he was a bit scared about moving back to Ross-more, afraid that someone would find him out. Especially Peter. He would have been one of the people to have known Barney best. But by that time Peter was suffering from Alzheimers.

'Albert didn't go out much at first. He let people get used to seeing the light in the house again, and the smoke coming from the chimney. Then he began to venture out more frequently. Some people may have thought they saw a change in him, but would have put it down to living a hard life away, without many friends. A man living alone in foreign parts often ends up morose and cranky.

'So Albert slid back into Rossmore society as Barney, and it worked perfectly – until the Cooper family came to Fernhill. Your questions,' nodding at Ian, 'frightened the life out of him. He may have though you had penetrated his disguise.'

'So that explains why he wouldn't tell me the old stories. He didn't know them. They were part of the real Barney,' said Ian.

'What happened about the silver mining?' asked Brian.

'The mining company lost interest. They said it would not be a viable proposition without Fernhill. It seems the vein of ore ran right through Peter's land too, but he had refused to sell. By that time Albert was settled back here so he decided to stay on. He felt that all he had to do was to wait for Peter to die and make the new owner an offer. He got a huge disappointment when he realised the Coopers had no intention of selling. But Albert is a very greedy man and he doesn't give up. When he heard that the Byrnes were disputing your right to Fernhill, he offered to pay all legal costs, on condition that they would sell to him – if the case was successful.'

'Putting us through all that agony' Sheila couldn't refrain from putting in.

'It also makes sense of something we thought very mysterious,' said Ian. 'Remember, Sheila, when we were here about a fortnight we got a letter asking if we would sell. We thought it was junk mail.'

'What will happen to him now?' asked Brian.

'Depends. I have my own thoughts about that.'

'What do you mean?'

'I think he's not the full shilling. The murder of Richard preyed on his mind.' No doubt about that. And keeping it bottled up all those years can't have helped. Then when he came back here and thought he had finally got away with it, along came the Coopers. First Ian with the questions. Then Brian calling himself Richard Grier.'

'I think you're absolutely right,' said Simon gravely. 'It's a classic case of a murderer being haunted by guilt. I have no doubt at all but that he became completely unhinged over the past few weeks. Who else would try and murder a boy who only *said* he was someone else? Parry had to think that it was truly Richard Grier come back to life to torment him and reveal his secret.'

'On that note I must leave you,' said Sergeant Coleman. 'Must get back and write up my report.'

13
Together at Last

In the evening, after a sombre day, there was a lightning of mood when Simon insisted on taking them all over to the hotel in Rossmore for supper. He was leaving in he morning.

Later that night, when Simon sat with Sheila and Ian in the sitting-room having a night-cap, he said, 'I think we can definitely say it's over now. I'll be making out a detailed report when I get back to America, and I will send a copy to the Society for Psychical Research in London. They may contact you at some stage for additional information.

They were all sad to see Simon go, and everyone was up in the morning to see him off.

'Thanks for all you have done for us,' said Sheila warmly.

'We'll be in touch,' promised Ian.

'It's been a remarkable experience meeting you, and I certainly will keep in touch,' said Simon, shaking hands all round. When he came to Brian he handed him the red-handled pocket-knife. 'I think you should have this.'

They all stood and waved, until the car was out of sight.

'He'll be back,' said Ian, putting his arm around Brian's shoulders.

Sheila and Ian decided that Brian should not return to school until after Richard was buried.

The morning of the funeral was cold but mainly dry, although there were flurries of snow by the time they reached Rossmore. The church was crowded, and Brian, Cliona and Niamh sat beside Laura and Michael. David and Kieran were in the seat behind. The congregation was attentive, as they listened to Father Lynch's moving sermon, and the children's choir sang sweetly as Richard's coffin, followed by hundreds of people, was wheeled from the church.

Later, in the small graveyard outside Rossmore, the friends stood together again, drawn closer by their shared experiences. With the rest of the mourners, they made

their responses to the graveside prayers as the coffin was lowered into the earth.

Richard was interred in the Grier plot where, years before, Susannah's wish had been granted and she had been buried beside her first husband. Now in death the small family was reunited again. Albert Parry had forever lost his hold on them.

As the priest shook holy water on the open grave, the wind grew stronger, the bare branches of the large sycamores that surrounded the graveyard bent and swayed, and the people shivered, turning up their collars as they huddled more deeply into their warm winter coats.

And then Brian heard it again, the sound that had once made his blood run cold. It was a sigh, much softer this time, but still it filled the air about him. Lifting his head in alarm he looked around at the other mourners, but they continued the steady response to the prayers. Obviously they had heard nothing.

He jumped when a hand gripped his shoulder, but relaxed again when his father spoke, 'Come on, Brian. It's over now. Let's go home.'

Large flakes of snow were beginning to fall as he followed his parents along the narrow path to the wrought-iron gates that led from the graveyard. He did not look back. After all, it was over now.

But back at Fernhill he could not settle down. He wandered restlessly about the house, up and down the stairs, unable to decide what he wanted to do. It was not until later when Laura called that he finally made up his mind.

'Will you come across to Ashbrook with me?' he asked quietly.

'Now?' she asked in surprise.

'Yes, there is still something I must do.'

Ian was just putting down the phone as they were leaving. 'That was Sergeant Coleman. He rang to say that Albert Parry died this morning.'

'I'm not sorry he's dead,' Brian said as they went up the lane.

When they reached Ashbrook, Brian paused for a moment in the hall, remembering his first visit, before going upstairs to the L-shaped room.

Simon and Ian had told him all that had taken place on his second visit, and he showed Laura the X through R.I.P., which left the letters R.G. showing clearly.

'That must make Richard happy,' he said, taking a plastic box from his inside pocket. He took off the lid and showed her Richard's blue diary and the red pocket-knife. 'I thought I should return the diary to where he always kept it, except on that last evening,' he explained, and going to the fireplace he knelt down and lifted away the piece of floorboard.

'So that was Richard's hiding-place.'

'Yes, and there's something else here too.'

Feeling around in the space, Brian removed a jar of coloured marbles and a wire-framed catapult, the rubber hanging in shreds, long since perished.

'I'll take a couple of marbles. I don't think he'd mind,' and taking out one blue and one brown marble, he carefully replaced the jar. He put the catapult into the plastic box with the diary and the penknife and, putting it back, he then replaced the floorboard. 'There, I feel better now, knowing there will always be part of Richard in this house.'

'It has been a very strange time,' he said to Laura, as they were going downstairs again.

'I know, but maybe it was all meant to happen. You were such an important part of it all. Richard or Susannah would never have wanted Albert to get his hands on Fernhill, so Richard was able to work through you to find the land certificate. It would not have been such a happy ending if it had not been found.'

'Yes. Funny, I didn't want to move here at first, and now I love it,' said Brian as they stood for a moment on the steps looking out on the neglected garden.

And then, in the still November air, a sigh could be heard, but this time it came from Brian, as he quietly closed the door, leaving the past behind, knowing that now she had at last found Richard, the ghost of Susannah Parry could finally rest.

Author's Note

Once again, my thanks to Maureen McIntyre of Glenties Library for help and assistance. I am also indebted to Paul Gallagher and Mrs Campbell of Letterkenny Library.

Libraries have always been part of my life. Living in the country, with limited access to great institutions such as the National Library, often the only pathway to knowledge of all kinds is through the local libraries. And what a marvellous job the librarians do!

A life-long interest of mine (probably inspired by my father) has been the paranormal, and I have read widely on the subject. The books I found particularly helpful when writing *The Ghost of Susannah Parry* were:

Lawrence Le Shan, *From Newton to ESP: Parapsychology and the Challenge of Modern Science.*
Raymond A. Moody and Paul Perry, *Life before Life.*
Israel Rosenfield, *The Strange, Familiar and Forgotten: An Anatomy of Consciousness.*
Ian Wilson, *Worlds Beyond: from the files of the Society for Psychical Research.*

The poem I quote in chapter two is *Bas* by Mairtin Ó Direain.

Yvonne MacGrory
October 1995

YVONNE MacGRORY is Donegal born and bred. Her maiden name was McDyer, and she is a niece of Father James McDyer of Glencolumbkille.

She trained as a SRN, and now lives in Kilraine, near Glenties, County Donegal, with her husband Eamon and three children – Jane, Donna and Mark.

Her interests are reading, particularly local history, and she also sketches and gardens. She likes participating on quiz teams and doing crosswords.

Her first book was *The Secret of the Ruby Ring,* which won the Bisto Award for the best first novel of 1991. It has been reprinted several times, and published in the United States by Milkweed Editions.

The sequel, *Martha and the Ruby Ring,* is set in Dublin in May 1798, at the start of the Rebellion

TERRY MYLER trained at the National College of Art in Dublin, and also studied under her father, Séan O'Sullivan, RHA. She specialises in illustration and has done a lot of work for The Children's Press. Titles include *The Secret of the Ruby Ring, The Silent Sea, The Children of the Forge,* the Tom McCaughren 'Legend' books, *Save the Unicorns, Fionuala the Glendalough Goat, Henry & Sam & Mr Fielding: Special Agents, The Witch at Batsford Castle, The Witch who Couldn't,* and the Cornelius Rabbit books.

She lives in the Wicklow hills, with her husband, two dogs and a cat. She has one daughter.

In addition to illustrating, she has written *Drawing Made Easy,* a step-by-step guide covering materials, techniques, perspective, composition, various subjects – faces, cats, horses, trees, flowers, birds, dogs …

Lucy, a rather spoiled eleven-year-old, gets a
birthday present of a ruby ring. Inside the little
box in which it comes is a message:
The secret of this Ruby Ring
Is that two wishes it can bring ...
Lucy twists the ring and makes her first wish. It
comes true, but she finds herself transported
back in time, to the Ireland of 1885.
At first she is intrigued by the strange upstairs-
downstairs life of a 'big house'. Then she
decides she wants to go home ...
'As her gaze came to rest on her left hand, she
gave a gasp of horror. Her finger was bare!
The ring was gone!'
The Secret of the Ruby Ring is the enthralling
story of a girl caught between two worlds –
her own world of today and that of the Ireland
of the Land League, evictions, boycotting, and
Charles Stewart Parnell.

BISTO AWARD FOR BEST FIRST NOVEL OF 1991

192pp   £3.95

Martha goes to her first dance, and is bitterly
disappointed. When she discovers that the
ruby ring she received on her birthday can grant
wishes, she makes hers – to go to a truly
magnificent ball!
The wish is granted but she finds herself back
in the Ireland of May 1798.
In a vivid tapestry of the life of those days, with
its dinners, balls, country visits and theatre,
Martha meets some of the leading personalities
of the day. And there is a certain Andrew
who is captivated by the charm of the
'cousin' from Donegal.
But in the background the storm clouds of
rebellion are gathering. As Martha, torn between
two worlds, hesitates to make her wish and
go home, events move to a dramatic
climax with the arrest of Lord Edward Fitzgerald,
leader of the Rebellion.
That same night, the ruby ring is stolen!

176pp   £3.95